"I wish you weren't afraid of me."

He hadn't meant to say that. Last night he had tried to convince himself that fear was the safest emotion between them. Looking into her eyes, he felt himself being drawn to her, unable to summon the strength to resist his own desires. Amazed, he found his mouth lowering to hers.

Her lips parted, warm and welcoming. It'd been so long since he'd allowed himself this basic form of human contact that a deep shudder went through him. Blood pounded in his veins. He should pull away, end this dangerous liaison before it was too late. But he couldn't. Not yet.

Tortured, he pulled his mouth from hers. "You don't want to get mixed up with me." He forced the words out. Feeling deprived of her touch, he strode out of the room.

But he couldn't stop the images storming his mind, the same images of a willing Jessica that had deviled him since he'd first met her.

Except now he'd tasted the sweetness of her lips...and he knew that one taste would never be enough.

REBECCA YORK

A *USA TODAY* bestselling author, Ruth Glick published her one hundredth book, *Crimson Moon,* in January 2005. Her latest 43 Light Street book was *The Secret Night,* in April 2006. In October she launches the Harlequin Intrigue continuity series SECURITY BREACH with *Chain Reaction.*

Ruth has twice been nominated as a RITA® Award finalist. She has two Career Achievement Awards from *Romantic Times BOOKclub*— for Series Romantic Suspense and Series Romantic Mystery. *Nowhere Man* was the *Romantic Times BOOKclub* Best Intrigue of 1998, and is included in their reviewers' "all-time favorite 400 romances." Ruth's *Killing Moon* and *Witching Moon* both won the New Jersey Romance Writer's Golden Leaf Award for Paranormal.

Michael Dirda of the *Washington Post Book World* says, "Her books...deliver what they promise—excitement, mystery, romance."

Between 1990 and 1997, Ruth wrote the Light Street series with Eileen Buckholtz. Since 1997, she has been writing on her own as Rebecca York. You can contact Ruth at rglick@capaccess.org or visit her Web site at www.rebeccayork.com.

43 LIGHT STREET

REBECCA YORK
Midnight Kiss

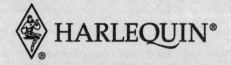

HARLEQUIN®

TORONTO • NEW YORK • LONDON
AMSTERDAM • PARIS • SYDNEY • HAMBURG
STOCKHOLM • ATHENS • TOKYO • MILAN • MADRID
PRAGUE • WARSAW • BUDAPEST • AUCKLAND

ISBN-13: 978-0-373-36062-8
ISBN-10:   0-373-36062-2

MIDNIGHT KISS

This edition published by arrangement with Harlequin Books S.A.

® and TM are trademarks of the publisher. Trademarks indicated with ® are registered in the United States Patent and Trademark Office, the Canadian Trade Marks Office and in other countries.

www.eHarlequin.com

Printed in U.S.A.

Directory
43 LIGHT STREET

	Room
ADVENTURES IN TRAVEL	204
ABIGAIL FRANKLIN, Ph.D. Clinical Psychology	509
INNER HARBOR PRODUCTIONS	404
THE LIGHT STREET FOUNDATION	322
KATHRYN MARTIN-McQUADE, M.D. Branch Office, Medizone Labs	515
O'MALLEY & O'MALLEY Detective Agency	518
LAURA ROSWELL, LL.B. Attorney at Law	311
SABRINA'S FANCY	Lobby
STRUCTURAL DESIGN GROUP	407
NOEL ZACHARIAS Paralegal Service	311
L. ROSSINI Superintendent	Lower Level

CAST OF CHARACTERS

Jessica Adams—She'd gambled her career on producing *Midnight Kiss.* Would it cost her her life?

Matthew Griffon—Dark, evocative prose was his trademark, and Jessica his obsession.

Perry Dunmore—The soap-opera star had a better offer and would do anything to take it.

Reva Kane—Jessica's efficient assistant apologized for eavesdropping and wanted to make amends.

Heather Nielson—Was the dewy young actress as innocent as she seemed?

Diedre Rollins—She'd survived one scandal. Was she willing to risk more bad publicity?

Edward Vanesco—Either he was trying to make a comeback or he wanted to put Jessica out of business.

Chapter One

The window rattled in its frame, and her whole body went rigid with a mixture of longing and dread.

Like a child afraid of nameless horrors, she burrowed farther under the bedcovers. "No. Leave me alone. I don't want you," she whispered, squeezing her eyes shut and tensing every muscle in denial.

For just a moment she basked in the potency of her resolve. This time it would be different. This time she would conquer the need to be with her midnight lover.

The barest brush of wings seemed to flutter against the casement. But she wouldn't look. She was stronger than he.

"Let me in, my sweet. Don't lie to me. Or to yourself. You know you want to feel my kiss."

"No." This time her protest carried less conviction.

His voice was a soft buzzing in her ears. His words pure sensation. Rich and seductive. Like a blur of coalescent warmth that flooded her with a sweet, enticing fire. Tendrils of longing wove their way past her defenses, coiling around her body, seeping into the very essence of her being.

With trembling fingers, she plucked at the scarf

around her neck. The scarf she'd tied in place to hide
the tiny marks that marred her neck.

His brand. On her flesh. On her soul.

"Come to me…"

The scarf fluttered away, forgotten. Throwing aside
the covers, she climbed from the bed and stood bare-
foot on the soft carpet, her face turned toward the
moonlight streaming in through the diamond-shaped
windowpanes.

"Please. I can't see you."

"You will."

Like a sleepwalker, she crossed the space between
them and reached for the latch.

One moment she was alone in the room, yearning
toward a phantom as insubstantial as mist. In the next,
he was beside her, real and solid. She stared up into
his eyes, needing to see the fire in their burning depth.

"At last, my love." His long, pale fingers combed
through her raven hair, stroked down her arms,
brushed tantalizingly across the gossamer fabric that
covered her breasts.

She moaned softly, holding out her arms to him,
feeling the strong throbbing of the pulse in her neck.
"I want you."

"Oh, yes." His lips teased along her hairline, across
her cheek, down to the warm hollow of her throat,
sending a stab of white-hot need to her core.

Stepping away, he reached for the tiny row of buttons that closed the front of her gown. Her flesh
burned where his fingers touched. She swayed on her
feet, feeling his gaze like a physical brand. Then he
swept her up into his arms and carried her to the bed.

In a kind of drugged haze, she stared at him through half-closed eyes, her limbs too heavy to lift.

Kneeling beside her on the coverlet, he pulled off his shirt so that he was naked to the waist. Then he took her small hand in his larger one and flattened it against his pounding heart.

"Feel how you excite me," he whispered.

Speech was beyond her. But it was a far deeper response that he sought as his hands and lips began to move over her body. She remembered this, the deep sensations that he aroused. The need beyond endurance shimmering through her being. Oh yes, she had craved this, even when she had tried to bar him from her bedroom.

"Ah, sweet, let me give you pleasure," he crooned as he took her to still greater heights. "The ultimate pleasure. Even as you give yourself to me."

And then his mouth was on her neck, and she felt a tiny stab of pain.

She winced, and he gentled her with his hands as he began to draw her life force into himself.

A SHIVER STARTED at the base of Jessica Adams's spine and traveled upward, ending with a tingling sensation in her scalp. Slamming the book closed, she set it quickly on the lamp table beside the sofa. Every time she got to the scene where the nameless woman opened the window to the vampire who was sapping the life from her body, she had the same reaction. Yet she kept coming back to the story. Coming back to the scene. Because she wanted to understand the author—Matthew Griffon.

Eight months ago when she'd confided to Sabrina Barkley that she was looking for the right subject to energize her budding career as a movie director, her friend had suggested that she read Matthew Griffon's works.

Right from the first taste of his brooding prose, she'd been hooked. Apparently she wasn't the only one. His evocative words were both fascinating and frightening—and had earned him a following that had put him on the *New York Times* Bestseller List again and again.

Jessica glanced at the hardback book, its shiny black cover adorned with a red, red mouth that showed the barest hint of fangs protruding from between the thin lips. There were no other illustrations—not even a picture of the author on the inside flap. The biographical sketch seemed designed to hide the facts of his life rather than reveal them. Matthew Griffon lived on a secluded estate somewhere on the rocky Maine coast. He was in his mid-thirties. And his first book had established him as a master of the horror genre. End of story.

Jessica sighed in exasperation. He wasn't even listed in *Who's Who* or *Contemporary Authors.* So she'd begun to fill in the blanks with wild speculations. Did he live in a crumbling gothic mansion with a dungeon in the basement? Did visitors mysteriously disappear? And what about the man himself? She turned him into the Phantom of the Opera—with a mask covering half his ruined face. Or pictured him with dark piercing eyes and black hair the way she saw the vampire in *Midnight Kiss*. More than once she'd superimposed the image fangs on the face she'd conjured up. Yet it was all fantasy—as insubstantial as vapor.

With a sense of inevitability, Jessica went back to his writing, his phenomenal ability to get inside the head of his heroine, his understanding of her longings and emotions. Every time she read his books, Jessica felt the power of his words, even though she didn't really know how he pulled it off. In fact, she'd been seduced just as effectively as his most naive reader.

Which meant she had an additional terror to confront. She'd gambled her directing career on the premise that she could translate the brooding atmosphere he created on the printed page into flickering images on a movie screen.

The chiming of the grandfather clock in the hall brought her back to more immediate concerns. Four o'clock already. And she was supposed to meet Richie Elsworth, her production manager, in Hampstead. Jamming her feet into a pair of running shoes and grabbing the script, she headed for the door.

The Scarlet House apartment she'd bought from Abby Franklin was within walking distance of her office at 43 Light Street. But it was a good thirty miles from the sleepy little Carroll County town where they'd be shooting *Midnight Kiss,* and traffic was worse than usual. Jessica hated to be late for appointments, and she found her hands tightening painfully on the steering wheel. Then she made a conscious effort to let the Eric Clapton song on the radio soothe her nerves, telling herself there was a good chance

Richie, who was coming from College Park, would be late, too.

An instructor in film arts at the University of Maryland, he was moonlighting for her because he wanted to see his credit line at the end of a theatrical release.

She understood the hungry feeling. Some people assumed the daughter of Cedric R. Adams, the legendary Hollywood director, would have it made. But she'd had to struggle for every break she got, and it wasn't just that female directors were few and far between. Sometimes she wondered if C.R.'s "old friends" were giving her a hard time as payback for his obnoxious behavior.

She had no illusions about her father. He'd had both the talent and the arrogance of an artistic genius—and the power to make his enemies wish they'd had the good sense not to tangle with him.

Well, Baltimore with its burgeoning film industry was a good place for his daughter to start Inner Harbor Productions. So far she'd paid the rent by shooting commercials for local companies. Now she was putting everything on the line with *Midnight Kiss*. It could make or break her career in feature films, which was why some of the problems that had cropped up already were keeping her tossing and turning in her bed long after Jay Leno had gone off the air.

The traffic thinned, and Jessica stepped on the accelerator after she merged onto the Northwest Expressway. As she pushed past the speed limit, she looked at the distant clouds. The sky had been grayish all day, and the March wind was still biting. Now the horizon off to the right was darkening to deep charcoal. Another good reason to get the meeting started quickly.

This was so different from the way her father had worked, she mused. C. R. Adams had had an enormous staff scurrying around taking care of details—while he pondered camera angles and romanced starlets. Jessica and her assistant, Reva Kane, did most of the grunt work. And since Jessica wasn't filming under the aegis of a big studio, she had to contract out for everything from film crews to costumes and makeup. Her only indulgence had been to lay out a small fortune for computerized editing equipment so she could work on the final stages of production in the middle of the night if she wanted.

Of course, there was one advantage to scraping along on a minuscule budget. Until her collaboration with Matthew Griffon, she'd also had the privilege of making all the decisions. And it was still a little strange not having final control of the script.

Twenty minutes later her attention switched back to the worsening weather conditions as she swung into the dirt and gravel driveway that led to the hundred-year-old Carmichael House—the Victorian mansion Richie had proposed for many of the indoor and outdoor shoots. After bouncing over a couple of potholes, Jessica slowed her speed to cross over a planked-wood bridge. The river below was a bit swollen from the spring rain. Would it make a good setting for an exterior shot? Maybe she could use it to show that a vampire couldn't cross running water so there was a chance for the movie's heroine to get away if she had the moral strength.

With her mind on location scenes, Jessica almost rammed into the car Richie had left at the side of the narrow driveway. Reflexively she slammed on the brakes, her startled exclamation momentarily drowning out the radio. After turning off the engine, she took several calming breaths before starting toward the house. The wind had picked up, and it whipped her chestnut hair around her face. Combing it back with long, graceful fingers, she stopped to take in the property. Richie had done a good job. This place could double for the Adams's Family mansion.

Her mind made quick assessments: Trim shrubbery, remove the old tree limb blocking the view of the front entranceway, paint the veranda and replace the loose shingles on the siding. She climbed the steps to the porch. At least the wood seemed sturdy enough there. On second thought, maybe they could leave everything alone except the tree limb and call it mood and atmosphere.

The front door wasn't locked, so she let herself into the mahogany paneled entryway.

"Richie? Richie?" she called as she crossed to the dining room, her eyes adjusting to the dim light. Her words seemed to echo around the dark, musty rooms like a distorted voice in a haunted house. She listened for a response but didn't hear anything except the low groaning of the wind. Yet she couldn't shake the feeling that someone was lurking in the shadows watching her.

Nervously her fingers skimmed along the top of a brocade chair and tangled in something sticky. With a little yelp of distaste, she pulled her hand back and peered at the clinging gray strands. Dust and spiderwebs.

Reva would have to get a cleaning crew out here before they did anything else. Could they charge it to the late Mr. Carmichael's heirs—who had sworn the place was in perfect shape for a movie set? No, that was probably pushing it. What she needed was a firm contract as quickly as possible, so the family wouldn't sell her set out from under her if they found a buyer. But she couldn't sign anything until she was sure the property was suitable.

Jessica scuffed her foot against a worn spot on the carpet. Damn, why couldn't anything be easy? Like why had her production manager disappeared when they were supposed to be having a meeting? Cautiously she took a few steps into the back hall. It was then that she saw it—the faint yellow glow of light shining up from the basement stairs as if someone had opened a door to the underworld.

"Richie, are you down there?" He didn't answer, and she felt the hairs on the back of her neck prickle. Every instinct urged her to back away. Instead she tiptoed closer to investigate. She didn't have to go down there, she told herself. She just had to take a quick look.

What she saw at the bottom of the steps made her heart stop for a beat and then start up again in double time. A body lay sprawled on the cement floor, the still form spotlighted by a flashlight beam.

"RITCHIE?" she quavered, focusing on his cropped blond hair, oddly remembering when she'd teased him about the unstylishly short haircut.

She wanted to rush to his aid, yet she stood gripping the doorframe as she eyed the stairs. Richie Elsworth was no klutz. Either the stairway was unsafe or— The only other possibility was that someone had pushed him. Remembering the feeling of being watched, she glanced nervously over her shoulder, but the hallway was as silent and empty as it had been a few minutes ago.

Jessica's teeth clenched. Richie's life might depend on what she did in the next couple of minutes. Cautiously she began to make her way into the basement, testing each step and listening intently for either a sound from the motionless man or a sign that she was about to meet the same fate he had. But the only thing she heard was the wind outside clawing at the shingles.

The first two risers were solid enough. When she reached the place where the third step should have been, she gasped and grabbed at the rail to keep from falling. Extending her leg, she felt around the empty space. Only a narrow portion of the tread remained. The rest had broken away.

Below her, Richie groaned.

"It's Jessica. I'm coming." She tried to hurry, her gaze fixed on his crumpled form. He was curled on his side, like a sleeping child so that she couldn't detect the rise and fall of his chest.

After what seemed like hours, she was finally kneeling beside him.

"Richie? Can you hear me, Richie?"

He didn't respond in any way, but when she gently touched the side of his neck, she was reassured by the steady beating of his pulse. Picking up the flashlight, she played it over his face and head. In the glow, she could see a lump at the edge of his hairline, and she remembered that you weren't supposed to move someone with a head injury. She didn't want to leave him lying there on the floor, but she knew he needed more help than she could supply.

"Hang on. I'm going to call an ambulance," she told him.

Before she left, she took off her jacket and draped it over his shoulders. Then she hurried back upstairs, scrambling over the missing tread.

She'd forgotten about the gathering storm. But as she flung the front door open, a strong gust of wind ripped the knob out of her hand. Trees thrashed around her like dancers in a violent ballet, and leaves flew past her face as she dashed toward the car. It was almost as dark as night, and she had to fumble to insert the key in the lock. Then, with a sigh of relief, she pulled the door closed behind her, shutting out the raging wind as she sank into the front seat.

She was reaching for the receiver of her car phone when a jagged fork of lightning shattered the sky. As she waited for the thunder to pass, a rush of movement to her right caught her attention, and her head jerked up. Looming over her, hand raised to strike a blow at the windowpane, was the menacing figure of a man.

As if in slow motion, his fist came down, down toward her cheek. Time snapped back into focus as his hand connected with the glass. It was a large hand.

Hard. Strong enough to crush her bones. For a split second she was paralyzed by fear.

He must have been in the house. He'd pushed Richie down the stairs. Now he wasn't going to let *her* get away. Frantically she dropped the phone and reached to press the door lock. But she was much too slow. He moved with the speed of a hawk diving to capture its prey. She could only stare at him as the handle twisted, and the door flew open.

The sky was as dark as pitch. The wind howled around them. Leaves and pieces of debris flew through the air, some of them pummeling the windshield and striking the fenders. But the fury of the storm had receded into the background. It couldn't compete with the immediacy of the solidly built man crouching over her, his dark eyes boring down into hers.

Time seemed to stand still as she looked pleadingly into their depth—trying to read his intent. The dark surface told her nothing, as if life had taught him to hide his emotions. But below that barrier, deep, deep where most people wouldn't see, was pain and anger. This man was capable of violence. And great insights, too.

She had the odd sensation that urgent messages were passing between them. Quickly. Silently. The intensity was too much—maybe for him as well, as if he knew he was giving away secrets. His lids lowered to shutter her view, and she was left with the rest of his face. It was strained, angular and lean.

He had come toward her out of the storm like a demon from a nightmare, his collar-length hair blowing wildly around his face. Yet this was no dream. As if to reinforce his power over her, his hand closed around her upper arm, his fingers digging painfully into her flesh. She gasped and tried to wrench away. "Please, don't—"

"Tell me what happened so I can help."

She went very still, unable to believe the urgent voice and offer of help she'd just heard could have come from someone with his harsh face.

"I'm not going to hurt you."

There was no reason to believe him, but his tone as much as his words stopped her frantic scramble to get away.

"Jessica, answer me. What happened in the house?"

She blinked. "You know my name."

"Of course I know—" He stopped abruptly. "I'm sorry. I should—I'm Matthew Griffon."

"Matthew Griffon," she repeated, still trying to get a grip on reality as she gazed up into the face she'd wondered about for so long. She'd gotten part of it right. Although there was no scar on his face, he *was* like the Phantom of the Opera, haunted by some dark secret. Yet he was no character you could describe in a few brief sentences. It might take years to unravel the complexity of this man.

"You came tearing out of there like the devil himself was after you." He gestured toward the front door that she'd failed to close behind her. It was flapping back and forth in the wind.

For a moment she'd forgotten why she'd come out to the car. "I found my production manager, Richie

Elsworth, lying at the bottom of the basement stairs. Unconscious. I have to call an ambulance.''

He let go of her arm and reached across her body, his hand brushing her knee as he retrieved the phone receiver where she'd dropped it.

She was still so strung out that the unexpected touch of his fingers sent a tremor up her leg. Hoping he hadn't felt it, she ducked her head toward the keypad and dialed 911. Static crackled on the line, and she waited tensely for the connection. Then the dispatcher answered, and she began to explain what had happened, concentrating on the answers to his questions. When she'd given the directions and her phone number, she hung up with a little sigh of relief.

''They want someone to stay by the phone in case they have trouble locating the address,'' she told Griffon. She wanted to ask *him* what he was doing here and why he had appeared like a chimera out of the swirling storm. She wanted to ask *herself* why she'd reacted so strongly to him. The questions would have to wait until later.

''I'll stay. You go back to Elsworth.''

''Thanks. I'm sorry I was so spooked. When the paramedics get here, tell them we're in the basement. And tell them to be careful. The third step down is broken. That's why Richie fell.''

The moment she climbed out of the car, the wind tore at her again as if it had been lying in wait like a wild animal. Another fork of lightning split the sky as she sprinted for the protection of the porch. Slamming the front door closed behind her, she hurried back toward the cellar.

When she reached the top of the steps, she gave a startled cry. The flashlight was where she'd left it—casting its eerie glow across the floor. But Richie had vanished.

Chapter Two

Jessica sucked in a ragged breath as she peered into the void. "Richie?"

For several seconds she heard nothing. Then a moan rose toward her from the darkness. It was followed by her name, gasped in a voice that was no more than a thin whisper.

"I'm coming," she called out, fairly flying down the steps and leaping over the broken riser. When she reached the bottom, she picked up the flashlight and swung it in a circle, keeping the beam low to the floor. Richie was slumped against the wall, his legs pulled up against his chest and his forehead pressed against his knees.

She crouched beside him, her gaze going to the lump on his head. "I found you a few minutes ago. You were unconscious."

"Yeah." His hand stroked across her jacket—which was now draped over his shoulders.

"I went back out to call an ambulance."

"I don't need an ambulance."

"Your head—"

"It'll mend." He gingerly touched the knot on his

temple and couldn't conceal a wince. In the distance Jessica heard the wail of a siren growing steadily louder. "You tumbled down most of a flight of stairs. You'd better let the medics check you over."

He didn't appear to be listening. "Stupid!" he muttered. "That was really stupid." He started to shake his head and winced again. "I swear, I don't know what happened. I was here last week and the stairs seemed fine."

Before Jessica could digest that bit of information, heavy footsteps crossed the floor above them. Then a broad beam of bright light swept the area.

"Watch out for the third step," Jessica called.

"Yeah. The guy outside told us."

Two white-clad paramedics came down carrying a stretcher. Richie grumbled as one of the newcomers examined the bump on his head. "I'm all right."

"Sir, your head should be X-rayed—unless you want to take a chance on internal bleeding."

He sighed. "All right."

"Do you want me to ride to the hospital with you?" Jessica asked.

"Are you kidding?"

She laughed. "Call me as soon as you get home."

"We can reschedule the tour of the house for tomorrow," Ritchie said as one of the attendants gestured toward the stretcher.

"It'll have to be Wednesday. I've got the cast scheduled for their first reading tomorrow."

"Jessica, we need to firm up this deal."

"We need to do a lot of things! But I can only be one place at a time."

"Okay. Wednesday." Ignoring the offer of assistance, Richie limped slowly toward the steps.

Jessica grimaced in sympathy as she watched him make his painful way up. He must have hurt his leg as well as his head. But it was obvious he wasn't going to let anyone carry him if he thought he could make it under his own power.

It took ten minutes for the group to reach the first floor. When Jessica stepped into the corridor, she looked around for Griffon. Was he still out in the car? Or had he disappeared as mysteriously as he'd arrived?

MATTHEW FADED BACK into the shadows with the skill he'd learned over the past few years. Through the tiny crack at the edge of the kitchen door, he watched Jessica follow the men outside. Miraculously the production manager was moving under his own power.

He shifted his weight from one foot to the other. Probably he should go out and make polite inquiries before the ambulance departed. But he'd given up on politeness for its own sake a couple of years ago. You didn't need it when you'd become an observer and recorder of life—rather than an active participant. Or when you made enough money to buy the privacy you craved.

The wind grabbed at Jessica's mane of hair as she stepped onto the porch. Her pictures hadn't done it justice. It was alive and vibrant like the wind. Involuntarily he reached toward her. Then the door closed, cutting off all contact, and he was left with a sense of loss—and isolation.

The second she'd come out the front door into the storm, he'd felt a jolt of recognition, and he'd known she was in a panic. So what had he done? Blundered up to the car as if he were an ax murderer on the loose.

He gave a twisted little laugh. Until a couple of months ago, his lack of people skills hadn't mattered. He'd been perfectly content living in the richly imaginative worlds he'd created. Making up fictional characters who became so real to him that he expected to look up and see them walk into the room. When his agent, Harry Tyler, had first forwarded Jessica Adams's letter asking if he'd be interested in negotiating an option on *Midnight Kiss,* he'd thrown it into the trash along with all the other requests he got from Hollywood types who wanted to capitalize on his success.

But she'd written again and sent him a tape of her best film—a love story called *Pete and Judy* that had shown mostly at art houses in major cities. It had been sweet and charming and surprisingly polished. And he hadn't been able to banish her haunting images of two wounded people reaching out toward each other. So he'd hired an agency to dig up a couple of her earlier movies—and watched them enough times to memorize some of the dialogue. After that, he'd started collecting information on her—telling himself that he was simply indulging his curiosity in a very intelligent woman who was going to end up being one of the best-known directors of her generation.

The next time she'd written, he'd kept the letter on his desk for a couple of weeks while he came up with a long list of conditions that would have to be met if he went ahead with a deal. He wanted to write the script. He wanted the set closed to the press. He wanted approval of everything from the music to the opening credits.

Ms. Adams had come back with her own set of requirements. She'd have a veto over his script. They'd jointly agree on the location, the music and the opening credits. They'd faxed demands back and forth, and to his amazement, they'd reached an agreement.

So here he was in Hampstead, Maryland, prepared to make sure his book got filmed the way he'd seen it in his head so many times. But he wasn't going to pretend that was the only reason he had come. Jessica Adams's work had intrigued him. Somewhere along the line he'd begun wondering *exactly who* had made those movies. Then he'd started fantasizing about meeting her—of sitting down face-to-face without the barrier of a fax machine between them. For the first time in years he'd let himself worry about whether they were going to get along.

Somewhere between watching *Pete and Judy* and negotiating the contract, she'd turned into an obsession. He'd be staring at his computer screen, but instead of the graveyard scene he was supposed to be writing, he'd see her oval face with those slightly slanted hazel eyes. The distinctive cheekbones. The mouth that was just a little too wide to be fashionable. The jawline that was definitely too aggressive for a woman. Not his type at all. Too assertive. Too much to say. Yet he hadn't been able to get her face out of his mind. Or any of the other physical details he'd learned. She was five-ten. Only an inch shorter than him. With long legs and— He pressed his teeth into his lower lip to stop himself from contemplating any of the other particulars he'd picked up from watching *Appointment in Taos,* the quirky and revealing little film she'd directed and starred in when she was just a teenager.

None of the personal stuff mattered, since he was going to keep things between them strictly professional. He'd told himself a thousand times that he didn't want anything from Jessica Adams besides her talent as a director. And even if he did, he was going to do her a big favor and keep his distance, because getting close to him would be dangerous for her health.

And speaking of her health— He crossed to the cellar door and picked up the flashlight that Elsworth had dropped on the floor. Then he began to play the light over the treads, stopping when he came to the one that had given way under the production manager.

As THE AMBULANCE drove off, a few fat drops of rain splattered the cracked driveway, and Jessica snapped closed the front of the jacket Richie had returned before he'd consented to climb into the ambulance. Maybe they were going to get a downpour after all. Caught between the house and the car, she tried to decide what to do next.

"Griffon?" she called into the wind, half wondering if she'd made him up, the way she'd made up so many other fantasies about him.

The sound of the front door opening made her jump

and whirl as he stepped onto the porch. This time he stood quietly with his hands in the pockets of his jeans. But he was no less dominating than when he'd loomed over her in the car.

"Where were you?" was the best she could manage.

He ignored the question, regarding her with an expression she would have called wary if she hadn't known better. From the moment he'd appeared out of the gathering storm like the villain in one of his novels, he'd had her at a disadvantage. As she gazed into his dark eyes, a twinge of her earlier fear came back, and her fingers closed involuntarily around the strap of her purse. She couldn't stop herself from thinking about the impact of his hand as it had smacked against the glass. From there it was just a short mental step to the frightening words he'd written on page after page of masterful prose. She shivered. This man had thrown her way off balance even before they'd met. Now she had to cope with him in the flesh. Out here in the middle of nowhere.

Michael Griffon wasn't that much taller than she was. But his physical presence was imposing. He must work out, because his body was taut and fit. She was less able to generalize about his face. She'd swear it had been made for warmth and laughter. Yet she sensed he rarely permitted himself those emotions. What she saw was a man who kept himself under tight control—as if he were afraid of the consequences if he relaxed his guard. Was he like this with everyone? Or just her?

"You're cold. Come inside."

"How did you know I was going to be at the Carmichael place this afternoon?"

"I persuaded Ms. Kane to tell me your schedule. And believe me, it wasn't easy. That's one protective secretary you've got."

"She's a lot more than a secretary."

Reva was handling the film's publicity and a number of other jobs. Like Richie, she was a lucky find for a director working on a shoestring. She'd been working for one of the country's top advertising agencies when she'd decided that she was burning out from the New York rat race. Because she'd put away a sizable nest egg, she could afford to take a cut in salary to work for a struggling Baltimore film company.

"It looks like you've picked some good staffers."

"Thanks." She lifted her chin and started toward Griffon. For months, questions about him had been simmering in her mind like a cauldron of witch's brew, and she wasn't going to let him distract her with a discussion of her staff. "I've been anxious to meet you. You write very evocatively—about terror and evil and desire," she blurted.

"I hope so."

"How do you get so much emotion onto the printed page?"

"How did you film the dream sequence in *Cat's Cradle* so that the images were like soap bubbles drifting around the room?"

Her eyes widened in surprise. *Cat's Cradle* was the film she'd written and directed for her Master's thesis, and as far as she knew, only a few prints had ever been made. "You saw it?"

"Of course."

"Where did you get it?"

He snorted. "You can get anything you want if you're willing to pay."

"But—"

"I'd be a fool to turn you loose with *Midnight Kiss* unless I'd looked at more than the film you wanted me to see."

"*Pete and Judy* shows what I can do."

"So does *Cat's Cradle* and *Appointment in Taos.*"

Jessica flushed as she remembered *that* amateurish effort. "I made *Appointment* with a bunch of high school friends the summer before I started at U.C.L.A."

"It was very revealing."

She felt her cheeks get even hotter as details from the plot came back to her. She'd been trying to prove how sophisticated she was by including a nude love scene filmed near the D. H. Lawrence ranch. Then she'd insisted on acting in the damn thing as well as directing. Had he known it was her when he'd watched it? And what had he thought?

He gave nothing away as he gestured with the flashlight. "Come back inside. I want to show you something."

This time she was glad to change the subject. Then, as she climbed the steps, she couldn't help wondering if he'd set out to embarrass her on purpose—as the most effective way to stop answering questions about himself.

But she didn't challenge him on that as she followed him down the dimly lit hall. Instead her eyes swept over the worn leather jacket that covered his broad shoulders and up to the dark hair that curled over the edge of his collar. He'd driven down here expecting to meet the director who was filming his book, but he hadn't bothered to dress up or even get a haircut. Which meant he didn't give a damn about making a good impression. She watched him move confidently through the shadowy house, as if he knew the setting intimately. How long had be been here? And what exactly had he been doing?

"I take it this is where your production manager met his Waterloo." Griffon's voice jerked her back to sanity. He switched on the flashlight and played the beam over the broken tread.

Jessica peered at the ruined step.

"There's another one that could have given way just as easily," he remarked, as if he were announcing something as indisputable as a drop in the barometric pressure.

She looked at him in surprise. "Which?"

He moved the flashlight, spotlighting the riser two down from the missing one. It was also cracked off, and Jessica drew in a startled breath as she looked around for the missing piece.

"When did that happen?"

"While the ambulance was leaving. I tested the rest of the stairs." Reaching behind the door, he pulled out a rectangle of wood that was lopped off along one long end.

He offered it to Jessica, and she turned it over in her hands, examining the surface and the edges. It seemed old and dirty—but solid. "It's a remarkably clean break."

"That's right. But there's no obvious reason why it gave way."

"Then what happened?"

He shrugged. "Don't know. But I'd like to hang on to it for a while, if you don't mind."

"Maybe we should show it to the police!" She was looking directly at him and saw his face go a shade paler. Or had she just imagined it in the dim light?

"I'd rather not get the cops involved," he snapped.

"Why?"

He hesitated for a fraction of a second before answering, and she wondered if he'd had a run-in with the law.

"Bad publicity."

"But what if—" She stopped and swallowed.

"If what?"

"Someone doesn't want this film made."

"What's that supposed to mean?"

She gazed down at the piece of wood in her hands, cursing herself for letting her nerves do the talking. The last thing she needed was to alarm Matthew Griffon. A couple of things had happened that had made her groan at her bad luck. But that was no reason to start making a key member of her team lose confidence in the project.

"I guess I'm letting my imagination run away with me," she murmured.

"I'd like you to be honest about any problems you've encountered," he growled.

"I didn't think you wanted to hear about every production detail. We've had some bad breaks. The film crew I was going to use backed out of the contract, and I had to sign up with a company I haven't used before. The museum claimed they never got our requests to film in their gallery. And somehow the copy of the script on my hard drive was erased. I had to reload the backup. That's all.''

He looked somewhat mollified.

She tried to take back control of the situation. ''I wasn't expecting you to be here tonight. But I have a progress report that I can send over to your hotel in the morning. If you'll tell me where you're staying.''

''I'm not a morning person.''

''Well—''

''You can give me some of the details now. I'd rather hear them in your own words than read a prepared statement, anyway.''

She found that while they'd been talking, he'd steered her toward the front door. As they stepped outside, she looked around, wondering where he'd parked. Only one car was in the driveway—hers. So where, exactly, were they going?

Earlier the wind had been fierce and the sky darkened by thunderclouds. Now it was truly twilight, and the air was as still and calm as the eye of a hurricane.

Griffon led her around the side of the house past towering azaleas and rhododendrons. When he started down an overgrown track that disappeared into a stand of pines, she hesitated as she peered into the blackness under the needled branches.

''I'm parked right on the other side. Next to what's

left of the carriage house.'' He gestured toward his left, but she couldn't see anything besides the trees.

His hand came up against her back, urging her between the pines. The unexpected touch of his strong fingers sent a little tremor down her spine. Or maybe she didn't like the way he was directing her into the blackness. She gave him a sidewise look, but it was too dark to read anything in his expression. She didn't want to appear uncooperative—not when they were at the beginning of what she hoped was going to be a good working relationship. Still she hesitated.

Suddenly he stopped, his whole body going very still. ''You're afraid of me.''

Her mind tried to form a polite denial. Her lips didn't cooperate. ''Yes.''

He took her by the shoulders and turned her toward him. ''Why?''

''I was afraid when you came up to the car like that. I didn't know who you were or what you wanted.''

His eyes kept her from lowering her gaze. ''And now?''

Almost against her will, Jessica began to quote from the passage she'd been reading before she left the house. '''She remembered this, the deep sensations that he roused. The need beyond endurance shimmering through her being. Oh yes, she had craved this, even as she had tried to bar him from her bedroom.'''

''That frightens you? Those words I wrote.''

''Isn't that the effect you want to give the reader? Or the reason you're so popular, for that matter.''

''I wasn't thinking of a reader. Or trying for mass

market appeal. I was trying to get inside the character's skin.''

She nodded. ''You didn't even give her a name. But when I read it, I...I could feel the evil pulling at her. She's going to be destroyed by her relationship with the vampire, but she can't turn away. She doesn't want to turn away.''

In the quiet twilight of the little woods, his fingers dug into her flesh. ''Did you ever feel like that about anyone or anything?''

''I don't know.''

''You'd know!''

''What are you trying to tell me?''

''Nothing. Forget it.''

But she couldn't drop the subject. She had to understand what was behind the mesmerizing characters he'd written. ''You have his feelings in there, too. The vampire, I mean. You make him...human. But you don't give him a name, either.''

''I wanted him to stand for a universal truth.''

The light had faded, and it was difficult to see Griffon against the dark background of the trees. But she saw enough. Despite the intensity of the conversation, the harsh lines of his face had relaxed a little, and she had the sudden insight that he felt more comfortable in the dark. Like a vampire. ''You feel sorry for him.''

''He doesn't like what he has to do. He destroys life, but that's his only option—if he's going to continue to exist.''

''The sexual quality to their encounters is unnerving.''

''It's not sexual.''

"Oh?"

"There's a difference between sexuality and seductiveness," he argued. "What she has with him is a substitute for sex."

"What is it for him?"

"A basic need. But not just for her blood. He craves her desire—her longing. He feeds on that as well as anything physical."

"But you said—"

"It's complicated. What's happening between them is very intense, something beyond normal human experience. But since she's human, she doesn't have any way to describe it except in sexual terms."

Jessica felt her heart pounding. He'd just said seduction wasn't necessarily sexual. Long before they'd ever met, he'd seduced her with the rich, evocative power of his written words. Yet his potency wasn't simply in his use of language. Now that he was here in the flesh, his pull was a physical force.

What did *he* feel now that they were face to face, this stranger who'd spoken so revealingly through his writing? She wished she had the key to decipher the codes he used.

His hand came up to brush against her cheek. Gently he touched her eyebrows, the bridge of her nose and then her lips.

Her breath went shallow, and her body swayed toward his.

"You're nothing like your publicity photos—or that brash teenager in *Taos*."

"How am I?"

"Fresh. Natural. Pretty."

"I'm not pretty. My mouth is too big. And my chin—"

His sudden laugh startled her. "Right. What do I know? I'm only a man."

She was glad the gathering darkness hid the red stain that sprang to her cheeks. God, why hadn't she ever learned to take a personal compliment gracefully? Probably because C.R. had been so brutal about her flaws. He'd been that way with everyone, not just his wife and daughter. But they'd been the ones who'd endured the sarcastic comments at the dinner table.

A jagged bolt of lightning and then a loud clap of thunder redirected her thoughts.

Griffon looked up, but thick branches hid the sky. "I thought the storm had passed us."

"The direction must have shifted."

"Then we'd better get out of here." Just as he took her arm, the wind came swooping back with a shriek that sounded like a chorus of doomed souls. In the space of a heartbeat, the night changed from still and calm to wild and angry. It lashed at them with a force that would have knocked Jessica off her feet if she hadn't reached out and grabbed a handful of Griffon's jacket. They swayed together until the powerful gust passed, then he tugged on her elbow.

"Come on!"

Icy blasts whipped at her heels and tried to tear the strap of her pocketbook off her shoulder.

As he led her through the swaying evergreens, Griffon hunched his shoulders and bent his head. Jessica crouched behind him. To keep from getting separated, she twisted her fingers into the hem of his jacket. She had no idea where he was leading her. When they rounded a bend, she wiped her hair out of her eyes and glanced around, trying to get a better sense of direction. Then a cracking noise barely audible above the howling of the wind made her freeze. Looking up, she saw a massive pine branch tear loose and come hurtling toward them.

Chapter Three

"Matthew! Watch out!" Jessica grabbed his arm, snatching him backward and off the path. The branch hurtled toward the ground, needles clawing at her hair as it landed in the spot where they would have been standing.

Griffon whirled and pushed her back into the protection of the closest tree. "Thanks. That was close."

She clung to the ledge of his shoulders, breathing hard and feeling as if he were the only solid refuge in a universe that had become dangerously unstable. He reached up and locked his fingers with hers, just as the heavens opened up.

The downpour was cold and sharp, the individual droplets driving into Jessica's flesh like icicles. She lowered her face to his chest just as another limb tore loose and came crashing down a dozen feet away.

Griffon wrapped his arms around her, pulling her securely against himself and preceding farther into the shelter of the trees. The fronts of their bodies were glued together like a label to a jar, and under other circumstances she would have pulled away. Instead she clung to him gratefully. As the icy rain pelted onto her head and shoulders, and the wind tore at her clothing.

She hadn't thought the torrent could get any heavier—until it began to hit her in drenching sheets that had her gasping for breath. For all she knew it had changed from rain to sleet, but her skin was too numb to tell.

MATTHEW STOOD in the fury of the storm, trying to shelter Jessica and cursing under his breath. He'd put her in danger because he hadn't been willing to let her leave. Now he had to get her out of the storm.

"Come on," he shouted, wondering if she could hear him above the wind and rain.

Matthew felt her nod against his chest and hugged her tightly for several more seconds, his fingers stroking over her sodden hair and across her icy cheek. He had the momentary illusion that simply touching her this way could warm them both—save them both.

Her teeth were chattering, her frame trembling. Gently he reached down and found her hand. When she knit her fingers with his, he felt something inside his chest expand. A little while ago she'd been afraid of him. Now she was giving him her total trust—and he was responding in a way he hadn't expected.

Turning, he began to lead her down the path, moving quickly but more cautiously than before. He heard another ripping sound louder than the wind, and they both stopped short. Somewhere to their left, heavy branches crashed and plummeted to the earth, but he couldn't see what was happening through the sheets of rain. All he could do was shield her with his body—

and hope to hell he was still going in the right direction.

"Damned if we do and damned if we don't," he muttered as he started forward again. Jessica hung on tightly to his hand and stumbled blindly behind him.

Finally after what seemed like hours, a bulky shape loomed in front of him. The camper. Thank God.

There were several seconds when he was afraid he'd lost his keys somewhere in the woods. Then his fingers closed around cold metal. Yanking the door open, he all but shoved her inside and followed on her heels.

As the door closed, she melted against him. He marveled at the sensation of holding her in his arms—and the sudden wonderful absence of freezing water beating down on his head and shoulders. Now the rain only drummed against the roof.

It was pitch-black inside. When he moved to reach for the light, she held him tighter, her body still trembling violently and her teeth chattering.

"It's all right. We're safe in here," he murmured.

"Where…where are we?"

"My camper." His hands moved up and down the sodden fabric sticking to her back as he pressed her closer, trying to warm her. Or was that only an excuse? Was he enjoying the contact too much? Sternly he tried to make his mind focus on what needed to be done. "Got to get this stuff off of you—before you catch your death of cold."

"Y-yes."

She tried to help as he tugged at her sleeves, freeing her arms from the dripping jacket. But her hands were trembling so much, he ended up doing most of the work.

She was from California, he found himself thinking. She couldn't take the cold like a guy from the Maine woods.

The jacket landed in a puddle at his feet. But he could tell she was no dryer or warmer than before. His hands stroked over her back and shoulders, feeling the way her T-shirt clung to her like a freezing second skin. Without thinking, he reached for the hem of the shirt and started to pull it up.

When his fingers brushed the bare skin over her ribs, she drew in a sharp breath. "Don't."

He stopped and jerked his hands away from her flesh. "Sorry. I—"

She swallowed. "It's okay."

He stood for a moment with his eyes closed, thankful for the darkness. Moments ago, taking off her clothes had seemed like the most natural thing in the world—as if they were old friends. Or as if they'd been lovers for years. But they couldn't be friends. And certainly not lovers. What the hell had he been thinking about?

"You need a hot shower—and some dry clothes or you're going to catch pneumonia," he rasped as he pulled away from her.

HE LEFT HER so abruptly that Jessica reached out to steady herself against the door. A switch clicked, then a weak light came on in the corner of the room. She could see Matthew's face only dimly, and she suspected he wanted it that way. She gave up trying to make out his expression and focused on his body. He looked as if he'd narrowly escaped a drowning. His dark hair was plastered to his head, and his sodden clothes clung to his muscular frame. She imagined she gave the same charming impression.

"The bathroom's this way." He led her down a short hall. "Put your clothes on the floor in the hall and I'll stick them in the dryer. There should be enough hot water for a shower...."

"What—uh—am I going to wear?"

He looked momentarily perplexed before turning and disappearing into the bedroom. Several moments later he reappeared carrying a navy sweatsuit. "This should fit."

"What about you? Y-you're as cold as I am."

"I'm pretty indestructible. All I need to do is dry off." After grabbing a towel, he left her alone.

As she took in the room, she blinked in surprise. She'd been in a few mobile homes, and the facilities were usually quite cramped. This bathroom could have been in a fairly luxurious house. It had a skylight—against which rain drummed—and a full-size tub instead of just a shower stall.

With almost numb fingers Jessica tugged at the metal button of her fly. It took several minutes to pull off her soaked clothes. Griffon had offered to dry them but she hesitated handing over her underwear to a man she barely knew. Then she shrugged. Better to just act matter-of-fact about the whole awkward situation.

The hot shower was like a magic balm, bringing her back to life, washing away some of the numbing layers from her mind. As the water sluiced over her body, she glanced at the door. Griffon was out there. Griffon who seemed to change so completely from one moment to the next that she couldn't keep up with him. In fact, she was so off balance she could barely stand.

She shook her head and reached for his spicy-smelling shampoo. She was overanalyzing when the best thing she could do was get to know him better. And the storm had given her the perfect opportunity.

Too bad Griffon didn't have a blow dryer, she thought as she spent several minutes working on her hair with a towel. It was still damp as she pulled on the sweats. The pants fit—since her hips were broader than her host's. The shirt made her look like one of the girls in *Little Orphan Annie.*

Wiping the steam from the mirror, she peered at her reflection. Every bit of her makeup was gone, and her hair was going to dry with as much style as a tangled pot of spaghetti. She felt her chest tighten—suddenly remembering the afternoon she'd forgotten C.R. was bringing home a photographer to shoot one of those charming "famous director relaxes with his family" spreads. She'd been playing in the spray from the underground watering system, her clothes sopping and her hair hanging limply around her shoulder. C.R.'s quick angry look had frozen the blood in her veins. But he'd pretended his daughter's dishabille was an amusing annoyance—until the visitor had left.

Jessica forced away the long-ago scene. She might literally look wet behind the ears, but she was going to be one of the best woman film directors in the country. No, one of the best directors. Period. And her job tonight was to convey quiet authority. Squaring her shoulders, she opened the bathroom door and strode down the hall.

Griffon was sitting at a long desk with a laptop computer and several other pieces of equipment—including a fax machine. He'd partially dried his hair and changed into fresh jeans and a black T-shirt that made him look more like a street gang member than a famous author.

His attention was totally focused on several sheets of paper he was reading, and it was apparent that he didn't hear her approaching. There was a red stripe down one side of the top sheet—which was the only thing Jessica could see for sure from this distance. She stood very still, regarding his chiseled profile. Her image must have flickered at the edge of his vision. He looked up, momentarily startled, as if he'd forgotten he wasn't alone in the trailer. Without glancing at her, he hurriedly shoved the papers into one of the desk drawers, locked it and pocketed the key.

Tensely she waited for some explanation. After giving her a long, appraising look that made her wish her underwear weren't in the dryer, he got up, carefully pushed in his chair and crossed to a compact kitchen area along the wall opposite the desk. Turning his back to her, he began to rummage in one of the cupboards.

Jessica pressed her lips together and somehow kept from demanding to know what he hadn't wanted her to see. Maybe he'd been reading the latest chapter of his novel while he waited for her to get dressed. Certainly that was none of her business. She stood listening to the rain pounding on the roof, wishing he'd say something. Even polite social chatter would make her feel less like a spy. But she had found out pretty quickly that Griffon wasn't the type for small talk. Maybe he'd been alone for too long. Or maybe he'd stopped caring what anyone thought about him.

"How does hot chocolate sound?" he asked, startling her with both his casual tone of voice and with the question.

"Good." Jessica watched him fill a small kettle. When he didn't contribute anything else to the conversation, she stopped staring at his back and swung around to survey the study. Maybe she could pick up some revealing details that would tell her more than his damp hair.

In addition to the desk, the room was furnished with a tan leather sofa, an easy chair and a thick beige carpet with a wet spot right in front of the door where they'd first been standing. Bookshelves lined the walls. Wondering how he kept the library in place while he was on the road, she walked over and saw that a narrow plastic rail ran along the front of each shelf. Each piece of equipment on the desk was also secured by plastic restraints.

While Griffon rooted around in the small refrigerator under the counter, she surveyed the book titles. A representative selection of American and British literature, as well as many of the more respected modern genre writers. Several worn leather-bound volumes turned out to be classic vampire stories—including Bram Stoker's *Dracula*. Her gaze dropped from the books to the desk drawer. She'd never been a snoop, but no one had ever practically waved a sheaf of papers in her face and then locked them away. Unable to help herself, she looked quickly over her shoulder. Then, bending her knees, she grasped the edge of the drawer and pulled, but it was locked, all right.

She had just straightened when she heard footsteps behind her. Had he seen?

He didn't comment as he set a plate down on the desk, and Jessica glanced at him from under lowered lashes. Outside when the wind and rain had lashed at them, he'd wrapped his arms around her and pulled her securely against his body. The age-old gesture of a man protecting a woman. When they'd first come through the door, she'd been trembling in his arms. The classic response of a woman leaning on a man's superior strength. But it was dangerous to take anything for granted with this man.

The intimacy had been replaced by an awkwardness that left her edgy, and she focused on the platter he'd brought. It held a thick wedge of what looked like Vermont Cheddar, a variety of crackers, apple wedges and a crock of salmon-and-cream cheese spread—all of which reminded Jessica that she had missed dinner.

While she cut herself a piece of Cheddar, he returned with two steaming mugs. She lifted one to her nose and inhaled appreciatively. "Sometimes, my mother used to fix hot chocolate in the evenings."

"For your family?"

"No. Just for me and herself. My dad said the phenol bromine made him jumpy."

"Was he a health food nut?"

Few of the people Jessica knew would have dared referred to C.R. as a nut—even if that had been their private opinion. But Griffon wasn't like anyone else she'd ever met. "Well, he liked a good steak as much as the next guy, but there were a lot of things he thought were bad for him." Jessica laughed. "Maybe that's why I eat everything."

"Umm."

The conversation dwindled, and for several minutes they concentrated on the food and drink. Perhaps Griffon was perfectly comfortable with the silence, but Jessica could feel it filling the little room and then closing in on her. "This is a pretty plush camper." She tossed the comment into the stillness. "You've got a lot of appliances and office equipment."

"I don't run them all at once."

"Where does the electricity come from?"

"A generator. But my storage batteries will keep the place going for a couple of days—if I'm conservative."

"Do you go on long trips?"

"I live here. So I can go where I want, when I want."

"But the book jackets say—I thought you had an estate in Maine."

He wrapped his hands around his mug. "It's not an estate, it's an undeveloped tract. That's why my loyal fans can't find the place when they come looking for me. My grandfather left me the land—and a falling down cabin on a bluff overlooking the ocean. I moved there after—" He stopped abruptly and looked away from her. Several seconds later, he picked up at a point that probably skipped a number of years. "I had this vehicle custom designed when I started getting royalties from my first book."

''Didn't you want to fix up the cabin?''

''A nor'wester blew it off the cliff one night. Luckily I'd moved in here.''

The silence stretched again. This time her host seemed as uncomfortable as she.

''I live about six months of the year in Maine. The rest of the time, I travel. All I need for my work is my computer and my printer.''

''So that's how you got such an accurate description of Santa Fe into your last book. You stayed there,'' Jessica guessed.

''Well, outside of town at a campground with electrical and water hookups.''

''What do you do to keep your fans from finding you—travel under an assumed name?''

''My real name.''

''It's not Matthew Griffon?''

''Matthew. Yeah. That was my middle name. I picked Griffon when I started writing.''

''Oh.''

He turned back to the food, dipped a cracker into the salmon spread and began to chew.

End of subject, Jessica thought, determined not to waste her breath doing any more prying. ''Thanks for the hospitality, but I'd better be going.''

''You can't.''

''Oh?'' This time she made it a question.

HE WATCHED the nervous motion of her eyes, and the tight line of her mouth. Yes, she hadn't stopped being afraid of him. He let the silence stretch, thinking that it would be better for her if he encouraged that fear.

And for him, too. For a crazy moment, he'd let himself get too involved. But this was a business relationship as with his agent, Harry Tyler. The only time he and Tyler had met had been at an isolated lakeside cabin in Vermont. After dark. With a few candles the only illumination so that Harry couldn't get a good look at his newest bestselling author.

He'd told himself he was amused at the man's reaction—and his reluctance to ask personal questions. To be truthful, it had been more like relief. Back then he'd been afraid that any questions about the author of *Midnight Kiss* would nip his fledgling career in the bud.

Seven years later, Matthew Griffon was too important a literary phenomenon for the dark secrets of his past to turn off his fans. In fact, in today's perverse world, his life story would probably guarantee a longer run on the bestseller list.

"Are you going to hold me captive here or something?" Jessica demanded.

He shook his head and gestured toward the rain drumming on the skylight. "It's just as bad out there as it was when we came in. You'd get soaked to the skin in a minute. And I'm not even sure how to get back to your car," he heard himself explaining. Really, he should let her go. What was she to him, anyway? Then he couldn't stop from remembering the way she'd clung to him as the elements had lashed them and the protective feelings that had welled inside him. They were almost as overwhelming as the way her body had felt against his when he'd first pulled her in here. Vulnerable. Achingly feminine. The skin of her torso had been so wonderful against his fingers. Silky smooth. Fine-textured. Soft. The tactile memory was embedded in his brain. He'd started to undress her, for God's sake! He still wasn't sure what he'd been planning next. Probably drag her to bed.

"What do you suggest I do, then?"

"Spend the night." *God, the lines of dialogue were coming from one of his books.*

"I can't—"

"You take the bedroom, I'll take the couch. I'm not going to make a pass at you." He turned away quickly before she could see how much it cost him to say that.

THE BED SMELLED like Matthew Griffon. Not just the spicy after-shave and shampoo he used. But the distinctive scent of his body—the scent she remembered from when he'd held her in his arms—permeated the bedclothes. Jessica rolled to her side and pulled up her knees, wondering how long it would take her to get to sleep. She should have let him change the sheets when he'd offered. But she'd wanted to get away from him as quickly as she could.

She'd felt the sexual tension crackling between them as he showed her the bedroom. But that wasn't the only thing that made her jumpy. She wanted to ask what he was hiding. Not just the papers in the drawer. What he was hiding in his soul. But the question had been impossible after the awkward silences that had broken their conversation.

Her gaze flicked to the closed door. She'd debated locking it. Then she'd decided that was a useless gesture. If he wanted to come in here, a lock wouldn't stop him.

She rolled onto her back, gazing up at the ceiling. There was no skylight in the bedroom. A vampire wouldn't want one there. Not when the sun came up in the morning.

The image on the book cover—the red mouth with the hint of fangs—flashed into her mind. Was that what he was hiding? That he was the damaged suffering creature he'd written about in *Midnight Kiss?*

She gave a nervous little laugh in the darkness. What a ridiculous tack her imagination was taking. He might write about humankind's age-old fears, but Matthew Griffon was as normal as she. Well, not precisely normal. But human. It was madness to think anything else.

JESSICA WOKE in the first gray light of dawn, momentarily disoriented before she remembered why she was sleeping in a strange bed in borrowed sweat suit.

The sound of the rain was gone. But something else had roused her from sleep. Something that played along her nerve endings like tiny pinpricks.

The dregs of a bad dream?

Lying motionless, she strained her ears. A barely audible flutter like wings at the window made her whole body go rigid. She knew that sound! At least in her imagination.

Her head jerked toward the noise as she tried to penetrate beyond the half-closed curtains. But she could discern only an indistinct ripple of movement.

Then another rhythm crept into her consciousness—

growing slowly louder and louder until she could make out the sound of waves crashing against a rocky shore. It was somehow familiar and it made a dreamy, peaceful feeling steal over her.

"Jessica. Jessica." The voice was like a soft buzzing below the cadence of the waves. My God, who was out there calling her? What did they want?

"Jessica, come to me."

"No." Mind-numbing fear engulfed her, and her hands curled in the sheets, as if she needed to anchor herself to the bed—to reality.

Words she'd read many times trailed lazily through her head only this time they were spoken aloud. "Let me in, my sweet. Don't lie to me. Or to yourself. You know you want to feel my kiss."

"No," she protested again, a fine sheen of perspiration blooming on her skin. She was caught in a nightmare—unsure whether she was awake or asleep.

"Come to me!"

"Go away." She burrowed under the covers, pulling them over her head like a child hiding from monsters in the dark. But the blankets and sheets couldn't protect her.

The waves pounded in her head, making her brain muzzy. And the voice kept up its silky insistence. As if her hand belonged to someone else, she tossed aside the blanket, stood on shaky legs and took a tentative step toward the window. Then another...

Chapter Four

"That's right, Jessica. Come to me."

On feet that felt like blocks of wood, she crossed the carpet.

Through half-closed eyes, she saw black wings fluttering on the far side of the pane, begging admittance. Small red eyes bored into hers.

"Let me in."

With tingling fingers, Jessica reached for the latch.

The voice took on a harsher, grating quality. "Yes. Open up to me. Embrace your destruction."

Her hand froze. Her eyes snapped fully open. For a terrible moment, she stared into the beady red eyes, the evil little face, the sharp white fangs on either side of the mouth.

"No!" From somewhere in the depths of her soul, she found the will to fight. Her arm drew back, and her fist crashed down against the windowpane.

As the creature flapped furiously against the glass, a scream tore from Jessica's throat. All she knew was that she had to get out of there before it broke through and got her. Flying across the room, she yanked the door open. Then she was tearing down the hall.

"Matthew! Matthew!"

The front door of the mobile home opened, and she stopped short.

Griffon filled the doorway. His hair was tangled. His shirt was off. Her gaze fixed on the long scar that slashed diagonally across his chest, making a track through the thick, dark hair.

"Jessica? What's wrong?"

Her eyes lifted to his face. "You…you were outside."

"I was checking the propane tank. What happened?"

He crossed the room toward her, and she felt panic rise in her throat as she backed away.

Griffon reached her in a few quick strides, his hands cupping her shoulders. For several seconds she stood stiffly. Then she let herself sink against him, her cheek settling on his shoulder. His arms came up to cradle her protectively.

"What's wrong?"

She dragged in a deep, shuddering breath. "Something was at the bedroom window. Just now. It woke me up."

"What?"

"The vampire."

MATTHEW STROKED his fingers through the incredible softness of her hair, so aware of her physically that he hardly knew what he was saying. "There are no vampires," he murmured. "I think my books have given you nightmares."

Her body trembled in his arms as if she were a bird

in a snare quivering with fear. But her voice was strong and sure. "No. I wasn't asleep! I opened my eyes, and I...saw...the bat fluttering at the window. Just like in *Midnight Kiss*. Its wings were beating against the glass—the way you said. And...and it was calling me. Asking me to let it in. Like the vampire calling the woman in the book. The same words, even."

He shook his head vehemently. "No!"

"I know what I heard—and saw. He said he wanted to destroy me," she whispered.

"That sure as hell isn't in the book. He never wanted to destroy anything!"

She lifted her head. Then her body went rigid, and he knew she was staring over his shoulder toward the open door. "You were outside," she repeated, only now he knew why that had upset her. "Matthew, you wouldn't, I mean..." The question trailed off, as if she were afraid to hear his answer.

"No, I wouldn't play that kind of dirty trick on you! Jessica, I wish you weren't afraid of me."

He hadn't meant to say anything of the sort. Last night he'd tried to convince himself that her fear was the safest emotion between them. But somehow what he'd been wishing as he'd laid restless and awake on the couch had slipped out.

She stepped away from him, her hazel eyes searching his dark ones. He wanted to look at something else, anything else, but she held him fast with her solemn gaze.

He said her name again, staring at her, sensing himself falling into those twin orbs. They drew him toward her, and he couldn't summon the strength to resist his own desires or the need to make her understand what he was feeling. Amazed, he found his lips lowering to hers.

The first touch was only a light brush, maybe because he'd known all along that it was the wrong thing to do. Or maybe deep in his soul, he was afraid she was going to pull away. But she didn't.

He caught the barest murmur from her throat and felt himself drowning in that tiny sound.

He angled his head so that his mouth could fit itself more intimately to hers. Her lips parted, warm and welcoming. It had been so long since he'd allowed himself this basic form of human contact that a deep shudder went through him. He knew she felt it, knew by the way her hands stroked over his naked back and across his shoulders, as if she were reassuring him that this was right.

The touch of her fingers against the hair on his arms sent a more erotic tremor through him, and he deepened the kiss as a thousand urgent sensations enveloped him. The intoxicating taste of her mouth. The provocative pressure of her breasts against his naked chest. The silky skin of her cheek against his. The little murmurs of approval she made deep in her throat.

His fingers sifted greedily through her hair the way he'd wanted to touch her ever since she'd come out of the bathroom with that beautiful auburn cloud around her face. His other hand drifted down, so that he could trace the curve of her waist and press her hips more tightly to his. She was only a little shorter than he, with long legs, so that their bodies aligned perfectly—sensually.

Blood pounded through his veins. He should pull away. End this dangerous liaison before it was too late. But he couldn't. Not yet. Not when his own pleasure and need were so intense. Not when he felt her responding to him as if she'd spent the night the same way he had—wide-awake, longing for this.

Just another few seconds. Another few minutes. Another half hour. This was why he'd come down here from his lonely lair—to hold her and kiss her. With unsteady hands he pushed up the hem of her shirt and splayed his hands against the warm skin of her back. No, he hadn't imagined how soft and silky and feminine she felt. The certain knowledge that he was about to drag her down the hall to the bedroom instead of out the door made him lift his mouth from hers.

Her eyes snapped open. "Matthew?"

"You don't want to get mixed up with me." He forced out the words.

She looked as dazed as he felt. And confused. "Why?"

"I'm a bad risk."

Her eyes begged him to explain. He shook his head and turned away. He waited for her to press him with more questions. People always had questions. That was one of the reasons he'd retreated to Grandpa's cabin after the police had satisfied themselves that he wasn't lying about the accident.

But she remained silent, her gaze turning inward, and he realized yet again how different she was from other women—other people. He dragged in a deep breath and let it out slowly. "I was about to take you outside so we could look around."

"All right."

All right. Just like that.

She looked down at her bare feet. "I think I'd better put on some shoes."

"Right. Maybe I can even pull on a shirt."

He wished at once that he'd said something else, because her eyes were drawn once more to his chest, and she reached to touch the scar that he'd carried for the past eight years.

"You were hurt," she murmured.

"An automobile accident."

"It must have been a bad one."

"Pretty bad," he answered tightly before turning toward the dryer. "I'd better get your socks."

After fetching her clothes, he stepped into the bedroom and crossed to the bureau and closet combination he'd copied from the specs for a ship's stateroom. When he'd pulled on a long-sleeved knit shirt, he turned and looked at the bed, picturing Jessica sleeping there.

It wasn't much different from the images that had deviled him last night. Except that now he'd tasted the sweetness of her lips. He stroked his hand across the indentation in the pillow where she'd lain her head, imagining he could still feel her warmth. Then he turned on his heels and headed back down the hall.

Jessica had retrieved her running shoes from the bathroom. He watched gravely as she sat on the sofa pulling on the socks, fiddling with the shoelaces, taking longer than was strictly necessary.

When she looked up and saw him regarding her, she flushed. ''I guess you can tell I'm putting off the moment when I have to step outside.''

Actually he'd assumed she was dealing with the fallout from the kiss, but he didn't enlighten her by disagreeing. ''Um.''

''I'm going to feel kind of silly if we look around and don't find a thing.''

''This isn't a case where a negative proof means anything. We won't be any wiser than we are now unless we find something.''

MATTHEW REACHED for her hand as they crossed to the door, and Jessica found herself holding him tightly because she wasn't sure what else to do. She'd told him only part of what she was feeling. And that was before the complications of the kiss.

She slid him a covert glance. It was safer to think about the two of them than the vampire. But their relationship wasn't exactly easy to figure out, and a few minutes ago it had taken an unexpected turn.

Something had happened between them. Something more than just a man and a woman who had met the day before and were attracted to each other.

Matthew Griffon was a man who'd locked himself away from the world. Before they'd ever met, he'd trusted her enough to let her do what he'd denied to scores of other movie directors—film his book. She'd been too gleeful about the coup to question his decision. Since their talk last night, she'd begun to realize he'd been as preoccupied with her as she'd been with him. Or was she kidding herself? Jessica gave him another look from under lowered lashes, wishing she were more experienced with men. But she'd been so caught up in her career for the past few years that relationships had been way down on her list of priorities.

She sucked in a breath and let it trickle out of her lungs. Who was she kidding? It didn't matter how many guys she'd dated over the past few years. None of her previous experience would have prepared her for someone as brooding and intense as Matthew Griffon. Someone who made you feel as if he knew everything going on inside your head while hiding his own thoughts as effectively as a cat hides in the tall grass. Then there was the kiss. He'd initiated it. Then he'd been the one to stop. So was she supposed to be relieved or miffed?

They hovered in the doorway of the camper, and she looked down at the damp ground outside searching for another focus for her thoughts. She could see his footprints leading around toward the right and then coming back, the second set scuffing over the first. She even thought she could tell where he'd been standing when he'd heard her scream. The dirt was kicked up where he started to run.

"The bedroom window is at the back," he said.

"Why is the camper so high off the ground?"

He startled her by grinning. "It's a special design—modified so I can carry a small sports car underneath."

"That's impossible."

"Money can buy anything—"

"—except happiness," she finished the aphorism.

"How do you know?"

"C.R. would have done it if it were possible."

They crossed a plot of mud and grass that hadn't been disturbed since the night before. As they approached the back of the vehicle, Jessica felt her tension mount. Disappointment surged when she detected nothing that resembled footprints.

"Do you see anything?" she asked, her voice barely above a whisper.

He drew her closer to the window and pointed toward a series of indentations on the wet ground.

They looked like animal tracks.

From a large dog? A deer? Had the bat wings she thought she'd seen been antlers?

Now that she knew what to look for, she could follow the path. One set of tracks led directly out of the woods. The other went back in again.

Silently she approached the ground directly under the window, staying far enough back so as not to disturb the pattern.

"Not a dog," she said. As she stared at the prints, a long-ago image tugged at her memory. But she couldn't quite bring it into focus.

"Not anything I can identify," Matthew added. "And I've seen plenty of animal prints around the trailer—in Maine and at various campgrounds. Everything from chipmunks to bears and moose."

Jessica bent toward the indentations. Each had a pad at the back and was divided at the front. Like—like— She grinned in triumph. "Like Bertha's."

"Bertha?"

"A goat. She belonged to Ramona. One of our

housekeepers, who thought that goats' milk was better for you than cows'.''

"You kept farm animals on Mulholland Drive?"

"How do you know where we lived?"

He looked momentarily startled. "One of those photo essays on the great C. R. Adams. Your house didn't exactly look like Old McDonald's Farm."

"It wasn't. We had one goat. And it was a big estate. The gardener built a pen for it in back of the garage. I used to bring her thistles and other stuff we picked in the hills and watch her eat them. Then Ramona got into a fight with C.R. and left. That was about par for the course with our domestic staff."

"Goat tracks," Matthew repeated. "Except that there's one thing wrong with your theory. A goat doesn't walk on two legs. Unless it's part of a circus act."

"What?"

"Take a close took at these sets. They don't come in fours the way an animal would walk—they come in twos."

She switched her attention from the individual prints to the pattern that stretched toward the woods and realized he was right. Right foot. Left foot. Right. Left. Right. Left. The pairs were about a foot apart. She kept pace with several sets and found the stride was about the same length as her own long-legged one.

"What mythical creature has cloven hoofs and walks on two legs?" Matthew suddenly demanded.

Jessica's head snapped up. "Pan. The Greek God of the Forests. Or the…the devil."

"Yeah. Well, I think whoever was out here this

morning playing vampire had his metaphors a bit mixed up.'' Matthew walked carefully around the cluster of tracks under the window, staring down at them and being careful not to trample any.

Jessica joined him. Hating herself for the need to verify an important fact, she walked to the far edge of the camper and looked at the ground. It was swept clean by the rain. Nobody had—She stopped and corrected herself. Griffon hadn't come around from that direction when he'd said he was checking the propane.

Letting out the little breath she'd been holding, she turned and found him watching her. The look in his eyes told her he knew exactly what she'd been doing, and she felt her face heat.

Quickly she stooped and looked below the back bumper. ''I see the wheels of your sports car.''

''I wasn't lying.''

She nodded and switched her attention to the ground. The area underneath the vehicle was just as muddy as what they'd crossed. In fact, it looked as if runoff from the storm had come coursing between the tires in a steady stream, carrying away surface silt.

But there was one thing under the bumper that didn't look wet—a black silk scarf about three feet long. With a little shiver, Jessica ran its length between her fingers, trying to imagine who had been holding it. Surely not a bat.

''What have you got?'' Matthew asked.

She handed him the silky length and watched him brush off a bit of mud.

''If this thing had been on the ground all night, it would be as wet as piece of seaweed. So I'd say you had an early-morning visitor, all right. Someone who can't decide whether they want to play Dracula or Beelzebub. "Damn! If I'd gone back out when you first told me about the vampire, we could have caught him."

"It's not your fault."

"Wait here. I'm going to see if he's still around."

"I'm going with you."

"Don't you trust me?"

"It's not that."

"Then stay here. It's safer, and your shoes will love you for steering clear of the mud."

Before she could answer, he turned and hurried toward the woods.

JESSICA STOOD with her shoulders pressed against the corrugated aluminum of the camper's side watching Matthew walk toward her. She could see from the way the corners of his mouth turned down that he hadn't found anything useful.

"Too many pine needles under the trees," he reported. "Maybe Daniel Day-Lewis could sniff out the trail, but I can't."

Jessica nodded. She hadn't expected another find like the silk scarf. But at least she knew she wasn't going crazy. Someone had been at the window. Someone who wanted to literally cover their tracks.

"Are any of your friends into practical jokes?" Matthew asked as he stopped beside the front door to take off shoes caked with mud.

"Not that I know of."

"Then we've got to assume the morning's performance was meant to frighten you."

"Not you?"

"He'd be wasting his time. There's nothing left that makes my hair stand on end."

"Oh?"

Griffon ignored her question. "Who knows you were meeting Richie out here yesterday? And that you didn't come home last night?"

Jessica frowned as she followed him into the mobile home. She didn't want to believe anyone she knew would have done it. Yet she realized she ought to give serious consideration to the questions. "Well, Richie himself, of course. Although I can't imagine he was in any kind of shape to come back here. You said you got my schedule from Reva. But it was general knowledge that I had an appointment to look at the house. If anyone tried to call me last night, they'd know I didn't come home."

"Or you weren't answering the phone."

"I always answer important messages."

Griffon stood in the middle of the study staring at the locked desk drawer.

"What's in there?" Jessica blurted.

"Papers I wouldn't want stolen." His words were clipped. He turned away and glanced across toward the kitchen. "We don't need to think about your morning visitor on an empty stomach. But I'm afraid I can't offer much variety for breakfast. Do you eat frozen waffles?"

Another quick change of subject, Jessica thought with a mental shrug.

"Waffles are fine. And coffee would be good."

"Well, you've stumbled on my one culinary obsession. I'm an expert on coffee," he said a bit too heartily as he pulled a coffeemaker from under the counter. In the freezer were several bags of beans. "What's your pleasure?"

Jessica selected Swiss chocolate mocha and watched him put them into a small grinder.

"You weren't kidding about being an expert. I usually grab a cup of instant."

He grimaced.

"I'm pretty sure it goes just fine with frozen waffles."

"All depends on your priorities."

The conversation stopped abruptly the way it often did with Griffon. Jessica watched him work, wondering if he'd ever had company to breakfast. Or any visitors, for that matter. Since there was no table in the kitchen, he must eat all his meals at the desk.

After setting down a tray of food between the computer and the copier, he settled his hips against the edge of the desk and stirred milk and sugar into his coffee. "Who's got a vested interest in your not making *Midnight Kiss*?"

"What?"

"Who are your professional enemies? Who wants to screw up your career?"

"Nobody," she said too quickly.

His eyes were intent on her face, and she felt her features stiffen.

"You're lying."

"I was thinking about all the people who hate C. R. Adams," she shot back.

"Who?"

"Directors he cut out of films they wanted to make. Actors he wouldn't use."

"Ex-wives," Griffon added.

"No. He stayed married to my mother...." Her voice trailed off.

"But?"

"There were always other women," Jessica said in a low voice. "That's why—" She stopped abruptly.

"Why you don't trust men," he finished for her.

"That's not true!"

"Why aren't you part of a couple?"

"Why aren't you?" She threw the challenge back in his face.

"We're getting off the subject."

"Are we? Well, I haven't made a big enough splash to collect enemies, but *you* have. Maybe somebody hates *you* and doesn't want to see your book filmed," she countered. "Who are *your* enemies? Who wants to screw up *your* career?"

"My career's already established. And I've just signed a new contract that will keep me in exotic coffee for the next fifty years. Turning *Midnight Kiss* into a feature film won't make much difference one way or the other."

"You're wrong. If the movie's a success, it will bring you millions of new readers—people who like the movie and want more."

He shrugged. "Maybe so. But it's not going to change my life much."

"Well, a lot of people are going to see it as another measure of your success, and some of them will be angry that they're not sharing your good fortune. Your agent told me you'd turned down a dozen offers to film your books. What if one of those directors or producers is nursing a bad case of sour grapes? Who asked you for an option on *Midnight Kiss* before I did?"

"I hardly think that Craig Kelly or Aaron Gold are going to waste their time getting even with me by tiptoeing around in devil boots. They're both too busy with other projects," he said, tossing off two of the biggest names in the movie business.

"You turned *them* down?" Jessica asked. She'd suspected he'd gotten some tempting offers. She hadn't known how tempting.

"That's right."

"Why?"

"They're both too caught up in their own vision. Even when they work from a book, the project has their personal signature."

"And you knew I'd be easier to control. That you could come down here and impose your will on me." The memory of his lips moving over hers and of his hands traveling sensuously down her body flooded back through her.

"No. I was impressed with your directing style, but I knew you'd respect my artistic integrity."

Jessica hardly heard him because the blood was drumming so loudly in her ears. She set her mug down so quickly that coffee sloshed onto the desk. "I—I have to go."

''You're not listening. Instead you're jumping to conclusions about me!''

''If you don't want me to jump to conclusions, give me some facts to work with. Like, for example, why won't you tell me what you locked in the desk drawer when I came out of the bathroom last night?''

A pulse thrummed in her throat as she waited for him to answer. Five…ten…fifteen seconds…an eternity.…

His jaw tightened, and she knew she'd been a fool to think that anything real could have been happening between them—when they'd talked. When he'd kissed her.

She felt a moment of panic when she couldn't recall where she'd left her purse. Then she remembered it had been on the shelf in the bathroom since the night before. With measured steps she retreated down the hall and retrieved it—somehow hoping against hope that when she came back the look in his eyes would be different. But Griffon was staring down into his coffee mug.

She wanted him to say something, to stop her from walking away. To tell her he hadn't been using her.

He added nothing to his previous exclamation. So she walked out the door with her shoulders squared, her head held high and her heart hammering in her chest.

AS SOON AS SHE WAS gone Matthew leapt out of his chair, crossed to the doorway and watched her head toward her car. Her stunning mane of chestnut hair was the last part of her he could see as she vanished among the pines.

He stood with his stomach churning—wanting to go after her. Wanting to explain why he was acting like such an ass. No, wanting to hate her for upsetting the even tenor of his life by asking for the rights to *Midnight Kiss*. Before he'd known anything about her it had been easy to shut her out. After seeing her films, he'd let his fascination with her cloud his judgment.

He clenched his hands into fists. That wasn't going to happen again. With jerky, graceless movements he turned back to the desk, unlocked the drawer and snatched up the sheaf of papers.

Chapter Five

His resolve to stay away from Jessica had lasted a whole twenty-seven hours, Matthew thought as he took a swallow of lukewarm coffee and tried to find a comfortable position in the Goodwill reject chair that squeaked every time he moved. The chair was in the vacant 43 Light Street office she was using for rehearsals. He glanced at her and then quickly into his cup before she noticed. When he'd walked in he'd been hoping— He chopped off the thought. He had no business to hope for anything from Jessica Adams besides a good job of filming his story. Still, he'd felt a void in his chest at her cool, detached look when he'd interrupted the rehearsal. She'd stopped the discussion and introduced him around. Then, before her cast could get sidetracked, she'd pointed him toward the coffeepot in the back and gone on with her meeting. No one would have guessed that Matthew Griffon and Jessica Adams were more than business associates or that she'd come alive in his arms yesterday morning like a camellia blossom in early spring.

SILENTLY HE WATCHED and listened from his seat at the end of the table. The lady director was going over some fine points of the script in her no-nonsense, all-business voice, and he couldn't help longing for the other Jessica back. God, what a contrast. Fire and ice. Restrained and wild. It hadn't taken much to make her the heroine in one of his fantasies…Jessie. He'd started calling her Jessie when he fantasized about her. The first time she'd been an innocent maiden who'd fled an evil sorcerer and ended up in his cabin in the woods. The next time he'd saved her from the vampire in *Midnight Kiss* and shown her she didn't need to turn to the forces of the darkness. God, what a laugh. With a mental shake he forced his attention to the rest of the cast. They weren't exactly unknown quantities, but today was the first time he could study them face-to-face. Was one of them the joker who'd pulled the nasty stunt out at Hampstead yesterday? Or were they dealing with someone else?

"Any questions before we start reading?" Jessica asked.

Edward Vanesco, the British actor who was playing the husband, cleared his throat. "Yesterday's run-through was quite illuminating but I think we ought to do a spot more with this first confrontation scene." His rich baritone voice had a commanding quality, acquired through years on the London stage. But Matthew noticed his hands trembled a bit as he made the comment.

Diedre Rollins, who was sitting to his right, firmed her lips. In the morning sunlight, the lines around her eyes stood out like embossed lettering on the cover of a bestseller. She looked a good ten years older than her publicity shots and twenty years older than the character of the wife in *Midnight Kiss*. He hoped the makeup man was up to the challenge.

"I'm not really prepared to discuss script changes at this time," Jessica told him.

Heather Nielson, the teenage actress playing the daughter, squirmed in her seat. "I understand, but like, you know, the girl's character isn't sexy enough. I'd pictured her more like a teenage Madonna." She tossed her long blond hair and batted her thickly mascaraed eyelashes at Perry Dunmore for effect.

Dunmore gave Heather one of the trademark I-don't-give-a-damn looks he'd perfected so well on *Restless Nights,* the daytime series that had made him the darling of the soap opera digests.

Matthew watched the byplay and wondered how he'd do as the vampire. He had the looks—tall, dark, brooding—and from all reports, a temper and a reckless streak to match. But this role was going to put his acting skills to the test.

"Were you volunteering for a nude scene?" Jessica asked Heather.

The young woman flushed.

"Then why don't you shoot for poignancy and nobility. Think Julia Roberts in *Steel Magnolias.*"

There was a ripple of comments and some snickers around the table. Jessica let it die down before she picked up the agenda. "Remember we're on a tight schedule and budget, which doesn't leave us much time for rewrites. For now, let's all turn to page one and go through the script again. And let's start putting in some of the emotion."

Matthew tried to look nonchalant as the cast brought his words to life. This was the first time he'd heard his work performed by others, and the experience was unsettling. It was strange, but as he listened he was getting a sense of why his audience reacted so strongly. He was also glad he'd stuck by his convictions. When Jessica had seen the script she had argued that they should give the characters names. He'd come back with reasons why he wanted to keep the format of the book. They'd faxed memos back and forth. When she'd come around to his viewpoint, he'd known he hadn't made a grave mistake in trusting her with his creative vision, after all.

Now his excitement leapt as Dunmore and Rollins went through the scene where the vampire first sinks his teeth into the neck of the love-starved wife.

Glancing up, he saw that Jessica was staring at him. His elation was mirrored in her eyes. *It's working! God, see how well it's working.*

A feeling of kinship swept over him, and he started to go to her. Then he remembered where they were and how they'd left things, and he knew from her face that she was having the same reaction. The intimate contact snapped. Wrapping his hands around his knee, he leaned back in his chair and tried to look like the unobtrusive author. But it was no good. For the rest of the session he was going to be as conscious of Jessica and her reactions as his own.

EXHAUSTED FROM the work session, Jessica swiped a stray lock of hair back from her forehead and shuffled her notes into a pile. For a second reading, things had gone pretty well. The members of the cast might not love each other, but they were all professionals, determined to shine in their parts. She'd just have to make sure nobody did it at someone else's expense.

"So which one do you think started yesterday with a little extracurricular acting-out in Hampstead?"

Jessica looked up to find herself facing Matthew Griffon. "I thought you left with everyone else."

"No, you didn't. You've been as aware of me as I've been of you."

His hands were shoved into the pockets of his jeans, as if he were relaxed. But they hadn't spoken privately since she'd left the trailer, and she could tell from his expression that he was waiting to see what would happen now that they were alone again.

She sighed. He was right. She'd felt silent messages passing back and forth between them since the moment he'd walked in the door. The rapport had been so intense that she'd had to remind herself of what happened every time they ended up alone. She didn't have the emotional energy to waste on a man who thought two people sniping at each other were having a meaningful exchange.

"Which cast member is only pretending that this movie is the greatest career opportunity since *The Bride of Dracula?*" he persisted.

"I don't know." She focused on the question. It was better than worrying about the two of them. "At first I was thinking about who might want to stab me in the back. Then I got too involved in the reading to think about anything besides the way the cast was interacting."

"You must not have very strong instincts toward self-preservation."

"On the contrary." Her eyes met his, and she could see he assumed she wasn't going to elaborate. Perhaps because she hated to give him the satisfaction of pegging her correctly, she went on. "Anyone who lived in the same household with Cedric Adams learned basic survival skills pretty quickly."

She had the pleasure of seeing his surprise.

"Are you saying he was as hard on his family as he was on his associates?" Griffon probed.

"I rarely saw him on the set, but my mother and I—"

Griffon's sudden sharp expression made her break off in midsentence. For a moment she was confused as she tried to interpret his obvious tension. Then she saw that he was staring at the door Heather had closed when she'd left the room. *Keep talking,* he mouthed as he tiptoed across the room.

Jessica followed the direction of his gaze, her ears pricked. She heard nothing, but she could see a shadow where the bottom of the door didn't quite meet the worn tile floor. As she watched, the light pattern shifted, but no footsteps receded. Someone was out there, listening to their conversation.

"You and your mother," Griffon prompted as he took another soundless step toward the door. "Or are you embarrassed to rattle the skeletons in the family closet in front of someone like me?" He might be setting a trap for the listener, but the challenge in his voice was real.

"Like whom?"

"An outsider. Someone who wasn't brought up in the glamorous world of Hollywood where dreams come true."

"Dreams only come true when you work your butt off."

"Are you saying you think you have control over your life? Over fate?"

Her heart began to beat faster, and not because someone was spying on them. Griffon wasn't just tossing off meaningless observations. He had told her something she needed to know, and she wanted to keep *him* talking. "How were you brought up?"

"By salt of the earth working-class people. By a mother and father who loved me and who would do anything to make their kid happy." He was no longer looking at her or at the door. And the expression of loss on his face made her chest squeeze with sharp pain.

Then he seemed to remember what he was supposed to be doing. His mouth tightened, and he began moving quietly along the wall toward the door. She wanted to tell him to stop. Wait. Give her a chance to find out something more about him. "What happened to your parents?" she asked quietly.

"Each man kills the thing he loves." Griffon bit off the words. The line wasn't his. But it was familiar— from a poem Jessica had read, but she couldn't remember where.

"Can't you answer a question straight out?"

Griffon had almost reached the door. The question hung in the air between them. Then in one smooth motion, he grabbed the knob, twisting and yanking at the same time. The door flew inward, and a woman practically fell into the room.

Jessica stared at her in astonishment, the thread of her conversation with Griffon severed as if a giant knife had cut through the air. The listener was Reva Kane, her assistant. The woman gave a little squeak of surprise and dismay as she toppled forward.

For a frozen moment, Jessica tried to process what she was seeing. Then she rushed forward. Griffon grabbed her arm before she'd made it halfway across the room.

Reva scrambled to her feet under her own power. Averting her eyes, she began furiously brushing at the streaks of dust that had banded across the bottom of her skirt.

"Are you all right?" Jessica asked.

Griffon began to speak before Reva could answer. "I think the more pertinent question is, Do you make a habit of listening in on private conversations?"

Reva flushed to the roots of her red hair. "I'm s-so sorry," she stammered as she turned toward Jessica. "I didn't intend to eavesdrop on you and Mr. Griffon. I thought everyone had left for the day, and I was going in to straighten up so the rehearsal room would be ready for tomorrow. Then I heard voices and I wasn't sure whether I should come in. I—I was trying to figure out who was in here."

"You could have tried knocking," Griffon pointed out. "That's the usual way to ascertain who's in a room."

"Well, you know how temperamental actors can be. Sometimes they're furious if you interrupt them in the middle of a scene. I mean, it could have been Vanesco and Rollins.''

When Griffon didn't look entirely satisfied, Jessica hurried to her assistant's defense. "It's been a long day. We're all a little bit on edge. And after what happened yesterday, Mr. Griffon is—"

His furious look stopped her in midsentence.

"And I'm not making a very good impression on him," Reva said in a low voice, brushing her hand across the bottom of her skirt again.

"No. Everything's perfectly okay." Jessica patted her shoulder.

Griffon took Jessica's arm. "Why don't we get out of your way."

"Yes. Let me get my things." She shuffled the papers into her briefcase and allowed herself to be escorted from the room. She hadn't planned to leave with Griffon but here they were together again, and she wasn't sure whether to be happy about it or alarmed.

He remained silent while she collected her coat from her office. As they waited for the elevator, he looked back toward the rehearsal room.

"Do you trust Ms. Kane?" he asked after the door had closed and the car began to descend.

"Yes. And if you're looking for a make-believe vampire with a connection to the film industry, it isn't her. She was in advertising in New York before she came to Baltimore."

"Then how does she know so much about the temperament of actors?"

"She's been with Inner Harbor Productions for

eight months. She's had plenty of opportunity to make those kinds of judgments.''

"How do you feel about her?" he persisted.

"She's been very helpful. Willing to go that extra mile for me. I think she sees my company as an opportunity to build up a prestigious, well-paying job with the advantages of living in a city like Baltimore. This is the first time we've done a feature film, and she's as anxious as everyone else to make it work.''

Griffon looked somewhat mollified.

The elevator arrived at the first floor, and Jessica exited into the lobby. *Last chance to escape.* "Well, here we are," she murmured. "I guess I'd better be getting home.''

When Griffon didn't reply, she took a couple of tentative steps toward the door. If he was willing to explore the provocative remark he'd made just before Reva had toppled into the room, she'd stay. But she was absolutely sure he wasn't going to pick up where they'd left off.

Griffon caught up with her and put a hand on her arm. "Don't go.''

She gazed down at his long, sensitive fingers, feeling their strength through several layers of fabric. He wasn't gripping her hard enough to physically hold her, yet his touch had stopped her in her tracks.

"Jessica, I'd like to have dinner with you.''

She lifted her eyes to his. "I never know what to expect from you. Are you doing that on purpose?''

"No.''

"You said you wished I'd trust you. But you make that difficult.''

"Why?"

"Every once in a while, you let your guard down. Then you're sorry."

"You're too damn perceptive—too analytical."

"That's what makes me a good director."

"Proving that to the world is the most important thing in your life, isn't it? You don't want to be known as the no-talent daughter of a Hollywood legend."

She swallowed. "I think you're every bit as perceptive and analytical as I am."

"You're wrong. I operate on a much more instinctive level. That's what's driving me so damn crazy." He turned to face her, his grasp shifting so that he was holding both open lapels of her coat. Neither one of them moved. In fact, she was having trouble simply breathing.

"Every time I'd look at you today, I'd remember the way your lips felt against mine. Soft. Welcoming. Then I'd want to reach for you," he rasped.

She'd seen that in his eyes. And if she were honest, she'd admit she'd been fighting the same impulses.

Her mouth went dry as she saw intent gathering in his eyes. Slowly, very slowly, he let his fingers slide down the fabric of her lapels. The folds of wool hid the backs of his hands, but Jessica was very aware of them. She drew in a sharp little breath as his knuckles grazed the crests of her breasts.

She knew he heard, knew he was as burningly aware of her physical response as she. The barest brush of his hands and her nipples were hard and aching. She should pull away. Slap him for taking that kind of outrageous physical liberty. Yet she stood rooted to the spot, her eyes unfocused, everything else forgotten except the feeling of hot anticipation gathering in her body as his hands slid upward again.

Behind her, a whooshing sound intruded on the very private moment. It took several seconds before she realized it was the elevator door sliding open.

"Jessica?" a woman's voice inquired.

Griffon's hands shifted slightly. He didn't turn her coat loose, but he moved so that he held the garment away from her body instead of pressing against her.

"Jessica?" The inquiry came again.

Jessica's eyes snapped back into focus, and she found herself staring at the familiar face of Marissa Deveraux. Marissa and her sister Cassandra were the owners of Adventures in Travel, a very unusual agency that had moved into the building two years ago. The Deveraux sisters could arrange anything from a Caribbean cruise or a group tour of the French wine country to an ice-climbing expedition in the Alaskan wilds. And they often personally supervised the trips.

Of necessity, Marissa was very good at sizing up unfamiliar situations quickly. With narrowed eyes, she looked from Jessica to Griffon and back again as if trying to determine whether her friend was in trouble. She seemed prepared to hang around until she found out if assistance was needed. "Are you okay?"

Jessica manufactured a social smile. "I'm fine. We were—uh—just hashing over a bit from the movie. You know. *Midnight Kiss*. Marissa, this is Matthew Griffon. Matthew—Marissa Deveraux, one of our resident travel agents."

The other woman's cheeks colored. "Oh. Matthew Griffon, the author of the book Jessica's filming."

He nodded and extended his hand. "Glad to meet you."

"Glad to meet you," Marissa echoed before making a quick exit.

Griffon waited until she'd left. "I think we can find a better place to continue this conversation. Do you have any suggestions?"

Jessica decided not to mention that they had gone a bit beyond the conversation stage. She also knew that she wasn't going to invite Matthew Griffon back to her apartment. Maybe she wasn't going to spend the evening with him at all. That would be the smartest course.

"I promised Richie I'd get back to the owners of the Carmichael property."

"I've already done that."

"What?"

"I called an inspection company after you left yesterday, and we checked out the house and grounds in the afternoon. Then I went over to Tom Carmichael's and signed the deal. You've got a two-month lease on the estate. At a thousand a month."

"A thousand? They wanted twice that."

"Well, since I'm coming up with some of the money for the production, I have a vested interest in expenses. I pointed out a number of problems—like the basement stairs, for example—and told them we'd make repairs and carry our own liability insurance. You've already got a policy, because that was one of my stipulations before I agreed to the project."

She didn't know whether to be angry that he'd outrageously overstepped his role or glad that he'd taken the problem out of her hands. "Your making the final call on the shooting location wasn't exactly in our contract."

"I know. But you were busy, and you were going to end up behind schedule if you had to spend much more time on the decision."

"I wish you'd consulted me."

"Next time I will." He looked thoughtful. "In fact, I'll even make a peace offering and start with the papers I locked in the desk drawer the other evening."

"Just like that? You're going to let me in on one of your secrets."

"After due consideration."

She let him escort her down the street to the Hyatt Regency and then up in the glass-enclosed elevator to the top floor where a restaurant called Berry and Elliott's took full advantage of the urban panorama.

Griffon paused as he surveyed the spectacular view of the Inner Harbor and the Baltimore skyline at twilight. "You know how to show a reclusive writer exactly what pleasures are missing from his life."

"Do I?"

His gaze went from the cityscape to her face and then to her lapels, and she fought a sudden breathy feeling.

"Matthew?"

Before he could answer, the maître d' broke into the conversation.

"Would you like a table for dinner?"

"Yes," they both answered.

They were led past the noisy happy-hour crowd in the bar and down several steps to a table along the window wall.

"Well?" Jessica asked when they were alone.

"You'll get what I promised. All in good time."

The response sent a little shiver down Jessica's spine. Was he referring to the verbal promise? Or their more physical communication? She wished it were easier to understand this man.

Above the din of voices from the bar, Jessica caught a snatch of the background music the restaurant was playing. The rhythm was a little like waves crashing against a shore, and she stopped, her attention fixed on the vibrations. She'd heard that sound recently. But where? A dreamy feeling stole over her, and she closed her eyes, drifting with the waves.

"Jessica?"

"Um...What?"

"I asked what's good?"

With an effort, she brought herself back to the restaurant.

"Is something wrong? You looked as if you were a million miles away."

"I'm—uh—just tired."

"Yeah. I don't know how you keep up that schedule. You'd better get some food in you."

Jessica focused on the menu. "Maryland crab cakes are a specialty. You should try them or the crab soup."

"You mean this isn't the kind of Baltimore eatery they show in the movies where the waiters cover the tables with newspapers and bring out steamed crabs?"

"Afraid not."

When the waiter came, Griffon ordered a Scotch on the rocks, a bowl of the soup and a small steak with a baked potato.

As they sipped their drinks, Jessica waited for him to comment on something besides the food, the view of the World Trade Center and the aquarium. He'd lured her here with a promise to share some information. But he didn't seem inclined to get to the point. By the time the soup arrived she was tired of whatever game he was playing.

"Have you changed your mind about the papers?" she demanded.

"No. I was waiting to see how long you could hold out before asking a direct question."

"Did I pass your test?"

"It wasn't a test."

"Then what?"

"I guess I can't resist teasing you."

Jessica felt her breath catch as she stared into his face, trying to judge the intent behind the words. He might have been spouting a facile line, yet she knew this man wouldn't waste his time on anything so superficial. "Teasing? Is that what you've been doing?"

He lifted his glass and took a swallow of his drink. "When I've got you alone, I find myself saying and doing things I shouldn't. It's almost a compulsion."

She wasn't sure whether he'd answered the question. "Why?"

"I can't help it. You know, I have the absolute conviction that I should do something unforgivable so that you won't want to have anything to do with me—

except so far as we're stuck in a working relationship.''

"Why?" she asked one more time, her mouth so dry she could barely utter the syllable.

"I like you too much to want to hurt you," he said, all traces of lightness vanishing from his tone.

"Why do you think you will?"

His face might have been carved out of granite. "Past experience. I told you, I've got a bad track record with…people I get close to."

"Is this what you consider close?"

He fiddled with his bread knife, and Jessica tried another approach. "Maybe you've learned enough not to repeat past mistakes."

"Maybe I'm making a mistake now. Maybe it's always going to happen, no matter what I do."

She wanted to lay her hand over his, but she knew that he had said more than he intended—and that he wouldn't welcome the physical contact. She looked down at her half-eaten bowl of soup. Then she heard it again, the music and the sound of the waves—and her mind went spinning off into never-never land.

Chapter Six

"Jessica?"

It took a great effort to pull herself back and focus in on the man sitting across from her.

"What?" she whispered, startled at the thin sound of her own voice.

"Jessica, you were sitting there for more than a minute with your eyes glazed over."

She stretched and yawned to shake off the lethargic feeling. "A minute? I couldn't have been."

"You were. What's wrong?"

"I was listening to the sea," she said dreamily. Far away she could still hear it, and she wanted to go there again.

Griffon was very quiet for several seconds, his eyes narrowed. "The music?"

"Um." She didn't really want to talk about it, and she was grateful when he turned to another subject.

"Let's go back to who could be trying to frighten you, and why."

"Yes," she said too quickly.

"You told me your father had professional enemies. You also said he had trouble keeping household help.

What about the staff? Did any of them have a really good reason to hate him?''

"You mean reason enough to go after his daughter fifteen or twenty years later?"

He shrugged. "Maybe we should talk to some of your father's former employees."

"About what?" She watched him pull a notebook out of his pocket and scribble something. "What are you doing?"

"I'm going to see if I can find out the names of people who worked for your family—who might hold a grudge against C. R. Adams."

"That's a little excessive, don't you think?"

He threw her a challenging look. "I think it's time to discuss those papers."

Earlier he'd made it sound as if he were going to do her a favor. Now she felt threatened, but she wasn't going to let him see that. "Good" was all she said.

He reached into his pocket and brought out several folded sheets. Jessica could see the same red stripe down one side that had been on the pages he'd locked up.

He handed them over, and Jessica realized they were fax paper. Which meant that the red stripe probably indicated nothing more than that he was getting close to the end of the roll when he'd received the transmission.

In boldface across the top of the first page was the name Perry Dunmore. Quickly she shuffled through the rest. Edward Vanesco. Diedre Rollins. Heather Nielson. Reva Kane. Richie Elsworth. Each of the actors in *Midnight Kiss* and the members of her staff.

"Why didn't you show me these before?" she asked.

"I'm not in the habit of sharing."

She gave him a long look before returning to the material. There was a short biography on everybody, going back to their date and place of birth. Then came schooling, dates of employment and credit information, along with more personal data—including arrest records.

Edward Vanesco had been hauled in for drunken driving three times and had had his license suspended. Perry Dunmore had been cited for possession of marijuana—and had had trouble paying off gambling debts acquired on several trips to Atlantic City. Heather Nielson had exaggerated her roles in the school productions that were part of her résumé.

Richie had been married at eighteen and divorced. He'd never mentioned his brief marriage—or the fact that his ex-wife was hounding him for child support that he found difficult to pay. Reva's résumé said she'd graduated from Rochester College. But she'd actually dropped out during her senior year. Last year Diedre had been branded an unfit mother in a nasty custody battle for her adopted twelve-year-old son.

Valuable insights, maybe, if you had a suspicious mind. But Jessica felt her righteous indignation rising as she read the dossiers.

"Vanesco and Rollins are old enough to have worked with your father. I should have checked to see if either one of them was ever in a C. R. Adams production."

"It wasn't in either of their credits. I would have noticed."

"Yet maybe they're hiding it. Maybe one of them hated his guts and sees an opportunity to take it out on you."

"That's ridiculous!" Even as Jessica uttered the protest she realized he could be right. Still, that didn't make her feel any better about the information Griffon had covertly collected. C.R. had sometimes secretly done background checks on actors, and she hated that sort of distrustful mentality.

"What gives you the right to pry into people's private lives?"

"I sure as hell have the right to try to figure out who's playing vampire."

"You didn't know anything like that was going to happen when you had these dossiers made."

"I knew there was the potential for trouble."

"Oh?"

"I believe in being prepared for all eventualities."

"I don't like this kind of preparation."

"You don't like what happened the other morning, either."

She swallowed but said nothing—wondering which one of them was being illogical. She'd already been upset when he'd pulled out the papers. Maybe the detailed information should have been reassuring, but they only made her feel like a voyeur.

It was apparent Griffon hadn't expected her reaction. Probably he'd assumed she'd be appreciative. His eyes were hard, challenging as they held hers. Then he slowly pulled another set of papers from his pocket. Still he hesitated before handing them across the table.

"You've got something I'm going to like even less?" she managed. "The really juicy stuff? Abortions? Sex change operations? What?"

"Nothing like that. But you'll react more strongly, I'm sure."

Jessica unfolded the sheets and found herself looking at her own biography. It was more complete than the others and had everything from her high school grade-point average to notations about her home life. There were even things she didn't know—like a couple of affairs C.R. had been carrying on. If it was true.

But why shouldn't it be? Everything else was right on the mark. Even her boyfriends were on record—including her first disastrous love affair. Mortification swept over her as she remembered the emotional energy she'd invested in Tony. She'd thought they were going to get married, and he'd simply been out for a good time—with C. R. Adams's only daughter.

She scanned the pages, seeing more things she'd have sworn nobody knew, things that she had *hoped* nobody knew.

"Why did you pretend to be surprised when I told you about how C.R. treated me and Mom?"

"I wasn't pretending. I was just trying to get a handle on your point of view—how you saw your family life."

"Oh, it was just great!"

"A lot of kids would have envied you."

She snorted. "Right. Because they only saw it from the outside. But don't change the subject the way you do when you want to weasel out of a discussion. I want to know how you got all this dirt. Did you hire a private detective?''

"Two detectives. One for you. One for the rest of our happy little family. And it's not dirt. It's research—which it looks as if we're going to need.''

"Oh? Has it led you to any sinister conclusions? Maybe I'm trying to sabotage my own production because I don't really want to succeed.''

"Don't be ridiculous, Jessica.''

"Me? You're the one who hired the investigator. You have a hell of a nerve prying into my private life. Or anyone else's.''

"I told you—I like to know where I stand.''

"This is—''

"Unforgivable?" he asked mildly.

"Yes." Pushing back her seat, she grabbed her purse and marched out of the restaurant.

JESSICA SEETHED all the way down in the elevator and across the lobby. As she stepped out the door of the hotel, a blast of cold air hit her in the face, chilling her feverish skin and making her mind begin to work again.

She strode quickly down the block, intending to cover the quarter-mile to her apartment as rapidly as possible. Instead she paused before she came to Pratt Street. Almost against her will, she stopped and looked up toward the restaurant. Most of the tables ringing the picture windows were occupied by couples or parties of four. But in the middle of the convivial scene she spotted a dark-haired man sitting alone, facing in her direction. At this distance, she couldn't make out his features, but somehow she knew it was Griffon.

She gazed up at the solitary figure, feeling his absolute isolation and realizing suddenly that he'd done exactly what he'd said he wanted to do. Something unforgivable. Something that would make it impossible for her to have more than a professional interest in him.

Yet maybe he hadn't planned it that way. Maybe it had been a defensive reaction to her anger.

Jessica stood rooted to the spot, gazing up at him, wishing she could see his expression. He looked far away and unreachable like a figure in a long shot. If she'd had a camera, she could have zoomed in on him. Mentally she tried to change the focus. There was no way to tell for sure, but she sensed that he was looking at her as intensely as she was looking at him.

The silent communion continued for several more seconds. Then she wrenched herself away. Shoulders hunched against the wind and hands clenched into fists, she headed up Light Street, listening to the sound of her own heels on the sidewalk.

Click. Click. Click. At first there was only the wordless sound. Then the staccato taps began to resolve themselves into a refrain. "Each man kills the thing he loves. Each man kills the thing he loves."

She shuddered. "Each man kills..."

Griffon had said that. Just before he'd pounced on Reva back in the rehearsal room. So much had happened in the short time since then that she'd forgotten all about it. She stopped and mulled over the phrase. She hadn't had any idea what he meant. Was he talking in metaphors? She didn't know, but she was pretty sure it had more than casual meaning to Griffon.

She focused on the words, seeing them in black type on a white page. All at once she knew where she'd read the line. It was the quotation at the front of his second book, *The Haunting of Greg Matthews*. The one she hadn't read much of, because the beginning had been too disturbing.

Shivering, Jessica wrapped her coat more tightly around her body. The book was about a young boy whose parents had been killed—changing his life in an instant. Suddenly the odd comment he'd made when she'd asked him for reassurances in the restaurant made a little more sense.

Absorbed in her thoughts, she hurried toward her apartment. She could feel the book pulling her almost like a physical force. Secrets were locked in those pages—just the way he'd locked the papers in the drawer. Only the book was something personal. His words. His emotions. Characters he'd invented to speak his thoughts. Not a set of factual reports from a detective agency.

Her anticipation was so intense that she barely registered her surroundings, until she began to sense a presence behind her.

Following.

Was Griffon trying to catch up? Had he come to apologize? Or to stop her? Could he have sensed what she had in mind? No. The man had a lot of talents but he wasn't clairvoyant.

Still, Jessica cast a glance over her shoulder, drawing in a small measure of relief when she detected nothing out of the ordinary. The other pedestrians on the street were all heading in the opposite direction. But the fear of being watched wouldn't go away. She'd felt this way not long ago, at the Carmichael house. After a few more steps, she stopped abruptly and turned all the way around.

There was still nothing. Nothing except a flutter of movement in the shadows surrounding the World Trade Center. It was as if someone or something had ducked behind the gate that led to the walkway along the water. Except that she remembered it was locked at night.

She had reached the open expanse of plaza that heralded the Aquarium. The cold wind blowing off the water lifted her hair, flinging it around her face so that it was difficult to see. Combing the strands off her forehead with icy fingers, she hurried on.

Something sailed through the air, colliding with her face, and she screamed, imagining a black-winged creature swooping out of the night sky.

Snatching frantically, she found she had captured a rumpled piece of paper that looked as if it had come from a sandwich. In fact it smelled like pickles and mustard.

"*Attack of the Killer Pickles,* my next major feature film," she muttered in self-derision as she squeezed the paper into a ball and tossed it into a nearby trash can. There were no creatures of the night. No phantoms in the dark besides the monsters of her imagination and the pretend vampire that had come after her at the trailer.

Still, all she wanted to do was get inside, out of the

wind and darkness. Unconsciously digging her nails into the palms of her hands, she picked up her pace until she was jogging along the sidewalk covering the last few hundred paces to her apartment building like a sprinter in the one-hundred yard dash.

The door to the lobby was only a few yards away, and she breathed a sigh of relief as she fairly leapt inside the door. When the desk clerk looked up inquiringly, she blushed. "I…uh…thought I saw a rat coming out of the gutter," she improvised.

"Damn things. Want me to have a look?"

"No. It's probably gone." Cutting the conversation short, she hurried to the elevators and punched the button. She was letting herself get spooked. But it was impossible to simply dismiss the sensation of being stalked. She didn't feel entirely safe until she'd closed the door to her apartment, locked it and walked through the rooms, opening closets and making sure no one was lurking there.

Nonplussed at her paranoia, she headed for the den, where her Matthew Griffon collection was piled on one of the end tables. She'd acquired the books over a three-week period. First she'd read *Midnight Kiss*. Then she'd had to go out and buy *Wings of the Raven*. Then *Last Train from Eden*. Each one had kept her up all night reading. Each one had made her feel the characters' hopes and fears so acutely that it had been like getting to know real people. And the maddening part was that Jessica never knew whether the author was going to make it come out all right. Damn him. He had it in his power to grant happiness to the people he created. Yet, as likely as not, he left them in despair. Or gave them only part of what they wanted.

But that hadn't stopped her from coming back for more punishment, she mused as she pulled *The Haunting of Greg Matthews* from the bottom of the stack.

The book seemed to tingle in her fingers, and she struggled with an attack of uncertainty. Stalling, she fixed herself a mug of tea and thawed a couple of blueberry muffins to replace the dinner she'd left on the table in the restaurant.

She ate the substitute slowly, but finally there were no delaying tactics left. After setting down her mug, Jessica made herself comfortable on the sofa and opened the book.

The quotation she remembered was on the first page. "Each man kills the thing he loves." Oscar Wilde. *The Ballad of Reading Gaol.*

Then came Griffon's first words. "After the accident, everybody assured Greg Matthews that he had been lucky. He never had the guts to tell them what he really believed. That he was living under a curse that would follow him to the grave and beyond."

Jessica felt her stomach clench around the tea and muffins as she read the paragraphs that followed.

The carnival had come to town, and ten-year-old Greg Matthews had begged his parents to take him. Finally they'd given in. And for an hour and a half, Greg had been in heaven as he'd ridden the Ferris wheel, toured the House of Horrors and stuffed himself with chili dogs and soda pop. He'd left his parents standing in line for the Whip and gone off to get a cotton candy when the disaster had struck. One of the cars on the ride was not secured properly. As it whizzed around a curve, it broke loose, sailing through the air and into the crowd of people waiting in line.

Four of them were killed. Including Peggy and Lawrence Matthews. Greg turned around to see the purple-and-yellow car plow into human flesh. Heard the screams. Rushed forward to try to get to his parents. Well-meaning hands restrained him. Kept him from reaching the broken bodies. But the sight of that runaway car streaking through the air and striking the crowd like a giant bowling ball knocking down a set of flimsy pins would be etched in his memory until the day he died.

Jessica stopped reading when she could no longer see through the film of tears that blurred her vision. The images and emotions were so vivid—starting with Greg's feeling of joy mixed with triumph when his parents agreed to take him to the carnival. Then came the magic of the midway with its sights, sounds and smells calculated to entrance a ten-year-old. The enticing spiels of the barkers. The colorfully painted booths. The sugary aroma of junk food. Only the screams of a few patrons on the Ferris wheel foreshadowed the tragedy to come.

And the horror. The fear. The guilt. Because Greg was convinced his parents' death was his fault. He was the one who had begged and wheedled and pleaded until they'd given in and taken him to the carnival— done something they thought would make him happy. And look how it had turned out.

"Oh God," Jessica murmured as she stared unseeing down at the page, thinking about the way he'd reversed the initials. "Greg Matthews. Matthew Griffon."

Was that really what had happened to him? Literally? Was that why he'd told her nothing in life was certain? Or was this book an allegory, a story in which fictional events became symbols for real ones?

It was almost impossible for her to go back to the narrative. But she forced herself to read on.

Greg went to live with his grandfather in New England. The old man loved the boy, but he wasn't equipped to cope with Greg's withdrawal from the world.

His grandfather. Hadn't Matthew said something about inheriting his grandfather's tract of land and his cabin in the woods?

In the story, Greg became more and more involved in a fantasyland he made up. Subtly, as the story progressed, the place became a separate reality—another universe more real than Greg's actual life. Then creatures from that dark world tried to use him as a bridge to this one, and Greg found himself fighting for the survival of mankind.

Jessica looked up, not really surprised that she'd been glued to the book for over four hours. The story had grabbed her by the scruff of the neck and dragged her along. It all seemed so real, although after the first few chapters she knew it had to be Matthew Griffon's fantasy. There was no alternate universe full of evil beings clamoring to cross into this world. But one section had made her grip the book more tightly. It was the part where Greg fell in love with a young woman named Gena. The two of them joined forces to defeat the evil invasion. In a scene as powerful and disturbing as the beginning of the book, Gena sacrificed herself to save Greg.

Feeling utterly drained, Jessica set down the volume. She wasn't finished, but she didn't think she could read any more now. Maybe because she suspected that the story wasn't going to come out the way she wanted. Greg was going to have to die to save mankind. She didn't want to read that part.

Her body was stiff as she pushed herself off the couch and walked to the window overlooking the harbor. The view was one of the things that had sold her on the apartment. Tonight she couldn't see the lights flickering in the blackness, only Griffon's haunted face.

When he'd been a little boy, he'd watched his parents die. She was sure of that. And later? Had there been a woman he'd loved? Had she died, too? In another freak accident where he'd been present? Or maybe some military action in a foreign country. Something violent, she was sure of that much. Was that why he was afraid to get close to anyone again?

She and Griffon were powerfully attracted to each other. But the evening had ended the way it always did when they started to get close. He'd done something to sever their growing rapport. Tonight, he'd almost cut the tie for good.

"I'm a bad risk. I don't want to hurt you," he'd said. That made a chilling combination with the line he'd used to preface the book she'd just been reading. "Each man kills the thing he loves."

''No, Matthew. No. It doesn't have to be that way,'' she whispered into the darkness.

It was very late. But she had to go to him. Tell him how she felt after reading the Greg Matthews book. Make him understand that there was nothing to fear from the intensity of the relationship building between them. It had been building since before they'd met. Since she'd first read his prose and felt its potency. And she hadn't been the only one. He'd watched her films. She'd sensed he'd wanted to know her as much as she wanted to know him. Then they'd kissed. Unable to stop herself, she felt the stirring eroticism of that physical contact flood back through her. Even now, almost two days later her skin flushed. Nothing in her experience had affected her like that encounter. But she'd been denying it ever since because she hadn't known where to go from there.

She glanced at the clock and then the phone. She had to make him open up to her. But the last thing she wanted was to give him any warning of what they needed to talk about. She had to see his face when she confronted him with her new insights. She grabbed her purse, then stopped in frustration. There was no way she was going to drive all the way out to Hampstead in the middle of the night unless she knew he was there. She had to call.

His voice pager number was in her appointment book. She dialed, punched in his ID number and followed the instructions to leave a message.

''Matthew, please get back to me as soon as possible. I need to talk to you. I realize it's late. But it's important. Where are you?''

A couple of minutes after she'd hung up, her phone rang. "Jessica?"

She felt a little surge of triumph. At least he'd replied promptly.

"Yes."

"It's after midnight."

"I know."

"You need to talk about something that can't wait until tomorrow?" His voice was guarded—as if he expected retaliation for the scene at the restaurant.

She kept her tone carefully neutral. "I'll be tied up with rehearsals all day again."

"Is there some problem with the production?"

"Yes," she murmured. In a way you could call it that. Anything that affected the two of them affected the production. "I want to come out to your trailer."

"Jessica, it's a long drive. And it's late."

"I know, but I'll be there as soon as I can." Instead of giving him a chance to protest, she quickly said goodbye and hung up and grabbed her coat. Bypassing the lobby, she took the elevator straight to the lower level of the garage where her car was parked.

Keeping her hand on the button that held the door open, she peered into the cavernous underground space full of cars lined up in numbered spaces. The facility was well lit—and about as safe as you could make a downtown parking garage. Security guards patrolled the area. The automatic doors were locked, and you needed to check in with one of the attendants before driving inside. But the feeling of being observed came back as her gaze probed the walkways between the vehicles. If she hadn't wanted to talk to

Matthew so badly she would have abandoned her plans and gone back upstairs. Instead she stepped from the safety of the elevator.

Her footsteps echoed loudly on the concrete floor as she headed for space 89. It was several hundred yards from the elevator and over in a corner—a location she hated, because she was always afraid she was going to hit the wall when she pulled in and out. So far management hadn't been able to give her an alternative.

Unconsciously hunching her head into the collar of her coat, she couldn't stop herself from scanning the area as she walked, so she was almost to the car before it became the focus of her attention. When it did, she came to a dead stop, and her heart started pounding in her throat as she stared through the side window. Either she was seeing some freak reflection in the glass, or someone was sitting in the driver's seat.

"Hey," she called out, unwilling to get any closer. "What are you doing in my car?" The intruder didn't move a muscle.

"You need some help, Ms. Adams?"

The unexpected question came from over her left shoulder, and she spun around to find herself facing one of the apartment's security guards. Tom Ward, his name tag said.

Jessica breathed in a gust of exhaust-tainted air and let it out in a rush. "Yes. Thanks. It looks as if someone's climbed into my car." She pointed, and the guard followed the direction of the gesture.

"You stay back, Miss." Ward drew his gun and began to tiptoe forward. Jessica knew she should obey his terse command, but it was impossible to stand alone in the middle of the cavernous space. Cautiously she tiptoed after the man.

"All right. Git outa there, buddy! Quick!" Ward reached the car and banged on the window. The man inside didn't move a muscle. Ward pulled the door open. With a sickening thud that seemed to echo through the garage, a limp body fell out onto the concrete floor.

Chapter Seven

Jessica gasped and jumped back. The guard seemed just as startled as she. Gingerly he knelt beside the man on the concrete floor and felt at the side of his neck for a pulse. "He's dead."

"Oh Lord." Jessica stared at the crumpled figure as the guard rolled him to his back. His hair was matted. A blond stubble covered his cheeks and chin. His fingernails were grimy and broken. But it was his face that drew her attention. His features were frozen in an expression of shock and horror that made her stomach lurch into her throat. She clenched her teeth and willed the sick feeling down.

"You okay?"

Jessica nodded tightly, rocking back and forth on his heels. "He looks like he's been living on the street," she murmured, forcing her gaze over his stained, grimy clothes.

"Maybe he slipped into the garage to get out of the storm."

"It's raining?" Jessica had been so preoccupied she hadn't been aware of the weather.

"Yeah, buckets."

She swung around in the direction of the exit. "How did he get in here? I thought the doors were secured."

Ward looked embarrassed. "There are ways around almost any garage security system. I guess he wanted a dry place to sleep. Bad luck that he picked your car for a bedroom. Was it locked?"

"I—I thought so, but I could have forgotten, I suppose."

"We'd better notify the police."

"Of course." Jaw clenched, Jessica peered inside the car. A man had died in there! In the driver's seat. Her stomach roiled again, and she doubted whether she'd be able to climb behind the wheel anytime soon.

The guard went to make the call, and she was left alone with the body. By slow degrees, she allowed herself to bring him into focus. He was a small, pitiful looking fellow who had probably had a hard life. Somehow it made her feel a little better that he wasn't anyone she knew. Or anyone she'd seen in the harbor area before. Under the grime, his skin was as pale as fine porcelain, as if— As if all the blood had been drained from his body.

A little chill traveled up Jessica's spine as she bent toward him. His head was turned to one side, and she could see something on his neck—something that pulled her closer.

Slowly she knelt. Almost against her will, she angled her head to get a better look. On his throat were two small puncture marks—one on either side. Two wicked looking little wounds that could have been made by the sharp, pointed teeth of a vampire.

JESSICA STIFLED a sound that was half cry, half moan. Scrambling up, she backed away from the body. Every instinct urged her to run and keep running. Instead she forced herself to take another look at the man's neck, hoping her imagination had somehow conjured up the wounds or that they were a trick of the lighting. But the blemishes hadn't gone away. They still marred the dirty flesh like two vicious jabs from an ice pick.

As she stared at them, a scene leapt into her mind. From one of the early chapters of *Midnight Kiss*. The vampire has denied himself blood for several days and finally needs to feed. So he steals a car, goes down to the docks where the homeless men live and pretends he's looking for a sexual partner. One of them agrees to come with him, and he drives to a deserted road where he immobilizes the man with his mesmerizing words and touch. After he feeds, he puts the victim in the driver's seat and pushes the car into a swamp.

"Oh my God," she whispered, her eyes pinned to the tiny wounds, her thoughts spinning between fiction and reality.

The guard came back and followed the direction of Jessica's fixed stare.

"You see something?"

"On his neck."

Squatting down, he took a closer look. "Oh, yeah. Kind of queer," he mused. "Never came across nothin' like that before. Have you?"

"No," she managed to say. Two days ago she'd thought a vampire was stalking her, but she and Matthew had pretty well figured out how it had been done. There *were* no vampires. They didn't attack Baltimore citizens—not even the homeless. They only existed in superstitious legends and the books of Bram Stoker, Matthew Griffon and a few other highly imaginative writers.

But if there were no vampires, why was this man lying dead on the floor of the garage with two puncture wounds in his neck?

"What do you think happened to him?" she asked.

He shrugged. "I don't know. Maybe he was an addict looking for a new place to shoot up. Maybe he overdosed."

"Drugs," she repeated, wanting to believe that, willing to take any sane explanation—instead of the recreation of a scene from one of Griffon's stories. The only difference was the ending. The dead man was in her car in her apartment garage instead of in a swamp.

"So what have we got here?"

Jessica was so caught up in her own churning thoughts that she hadn't seen a city police car arrive. The question was asked by an Officer Werner, a blond blue-eyed man who looked as if he'd be more at home in a Prussian army uniform than one from the Baltimore Police Department.

"Vagrant. Died in one of the cars," the security guard supplied in clipped phrases. "Haven't seen him in the vicinity before. Could be an addict."

Jessica was impressed with the terse explanation. She couldn't have dredged up anything half as succinct and to the point.

"Your vehicle?" Werner asked her.

"Yes."

"Well, the detectives will need to ask you some questions."

"Why?"

"We've got to treat this as a homicide investigation."

"You...you think he was murdered?"

"That's always the assumption with an unidentified body—until we come up with another explanation."

Jessica was asked to wait while the official investigation rolled on. Two detectives arrived within the half hour, and she supposed she should be paying attention to the details so she could use them for authenticity in *Midnight Kiss*. But she was too shaken for anything that constructive.

The best she could do was respond to the questions asked by the detective who'd introduced himself as Filmore.

"Why did you come down to the garage at this time of night, ma'am? Did the guard call you?"

"No. I was on my way to a business appointment."

Filmore raised his eyebrows. "What business are you in, ma'am?"

"I'm a movie director—with my own production company. I've been busy all day with rehearsals, and this was the first opportunity the author of the script and I had to confer."

Filmore took it down. "The author's name?"

"Matthew Griffon."

Apparently the detective wasn't much into the horror genre, because he dropped the subject and went back to questions about the victim. "You know him? Seen him before?"

She shook her head, wishing she could at least get out of the garage. Away from the body. Couldn't they do this somewhere else?

"Any idea why he picked your vehicle?"

"I don't know. It was in the corner. Maybe he thought no one would see him."

The crime scene crew arrived, and Filmore went to confer with the newcomers. Jessica slumped against the fender of the nearest car. When a new sound invaded the cavernous garage, she realized she was hearing tires squealing on the concrete. She looked up in time to see a small silver sports car careening around the corner, missing one of the concrete posts by inches. It bounced to a stop in back of the ambulance that had arrived earlier.

"Hey. This area's supposed to be secured." Filmore left the official group and trotted toward the intruder.

Griffon barreled around the ambulance.

"Just a moment, sir."

"Matthew!" Jessica breathed.

"Are you all right?" he asked, ignoring the detective and closing the distance between himself and Jessica.

"Do you have official business here?" Filmore tried again as he stepped to block his path. But Griffon detoured around him. Once again, he headed straight toward Jessica, his eyes never wavering from her. When he took her by the shoulders, she let out a little shuddering sigh. Then his arms were around her, gathering her close.

Until the first contact of his flesh against hers, she

hadn't realized how much she needed to be comforted. Held. By someone who cared.

Because he did care. No matter how much he had tried to hide it, she knew it now.

"Thank you," she whispered. "Thank you for coming."

"Are you all right?" he repeated, pulling her closer. His voice was an octave lower and several degrees rougher than she'd heard before. His fingers stroked over her shoulders, her hair, her face, transmitting important messages. Intimate messages. As if they were the only two people in a vast wasteland, and they had finally found each other.

"Yes." She wanted to close her eyes and do nothing more than exist in the circle of his arms. In a space that small. But she couldn't make sense of his arrival. Cocking her head back, she searched his eyes. "How...did you get here?"

"In that little sports job I keep under the camper. Sometimes it comes in real handy. I was waiting for you, wondering what you wanted to talk about." He stopped abruptly. "When you didn't show up, I called your apartment and got your answering machine. Then I started listening to the police band. They said there was a dead man in a car. With your license number."

Until now, Jessica had managed to stay in control. Without warning, tears gathered in her eyes, tears she couldn't prevent from spilling down her cheeks. "It was awful," she whispered. "I came down here, and he was sitting behind the wheel, and I didn't know who he was. Then when Mr. Ward opened the door, he fell out on the floor like a sack of—of—" The cliché potatoes had leapt to her mind. Somehow that was more heart-wrenching, as if the man's life had been worth no more than a bag of produce.

"And they've kept you hanging around the whole time," he grated. "God, I wish I'd gotten here sooner. We're going upstairs." He took her by the shoulder.

"You're not going anywhere until you tell me what you're doing here, buddy," Filmore interjected.

Jessica looked up, startled. As soon as she'd started talking to Matthew, the rest of the world had gone away.

"I'm Matthew Griffon. I was supposed to have a conference with Miss Adams this evening. Officer Werner was kind enough to let me into the garage."

"Oh, yeah? Well, I'll want to ask you some questions."

"I'll be in Ms. Adams's apartment."

The two men stared at each other. Filmore had the authority to detain them, but he must have seen something in Griffon's eyes that made him back off.

"Make sure I can find you there," he growled. Then he wheeled and returned to the waiting ambulance attendants.

Jessica's mind had gone white. Like white noise. No sound. No thought. If she started to think, she'd be in a world where someone had thrown out all the safe, comfortable rules. She let Griffon lead her to the elevator. He punched the right button and when they got out on her floor, he escorted her to her door, all of it as if he'd been here a hundred times before.

She stood uncertainly in the middle of her living room. It was Griffon who led her to the couch. Griffon who asked where to find some liquor and then rummaged in the cabinet at the base of her wall unit. Griffon who came back with a juice glass that he'd half filled with brandy that some client had sent her last Christmas.

"Sorry I couldn't find a snifter."

"I don't have any."

She smelled the brandy as he sat down beside her and lifted the glass to her mouth.

"Drink."

Obediently she took a swallow, recoiling at the fiery sensation. Her eyes watered again. "I—"

"Drink some more."

She took another couple of sips.

Griffon seemed satisfied and put the glass on the coffee table.

"Did you see him?" she whispered.

"The dead man? No. I was only looking at you."

"I can't forget the…the expression on his face. He was afraid of something. Horrified."

He waited quietly, as if he knew that wasn't the worst.

"And there…there were puncture wounds on his neck. Mr. Ward thought it might have been from drugs. But they looked too big to be from a hypodermic."

"Are you sure?"

"I saw them! They were like—like—" She couldn't bring herself to say it.

"The tooth marks made by a vampire?" he finished for her.

She nodded.

He muttered a sound that was part curse, part growl. Then he was standing up, pacing to the window and back again.

"It was like the scene in *Midnight Kiss,* when he picks up the homeless man and takes him for a last ride."

"Is that what you're thinking about? My damn book?"

"Yes"

"I've made vampires seem very real. Too real. And not just to you, apparently."

She nodded again, huddling on the couch.

"The medical examiner will do an autopsy. Don't let your mind spin off into fantasyland until you have some real evidence."

Before she could answer, the doorbell rang.

"It's probably that pompous ass Filmore," Griffon growled. "Checking up on us."

He was right. The detective had come upstairs to ask Griffon where he'd been that evening.

Closing her eyes and leaning back into the cushions Jessica let the two men do most of the talking. Finally Filmore left, and Griffon turned back to her. "You need some sleep."

"Fat chance."

"At least lie down. What kind of music do you listen to when you want to relax?"

"Not music. I've got some tapes my mother made when I was a kid. One had waves crashing against the beach. Like when the vampire was calling me." She stopped abruptly, her body cold all over. "What did I just say?"

"You said it had waves crashing against the beach—like when the vampire was calling you."

"My God. Now I remember! I heard the waves that morning, and they made me feel dreamy and peaceful. Then when the voice called me, I got out of bed and went to the window." She looked up at him, frightened.

He came down beside her on the couch and took her hand. Without conscious thought, she turned her palm up and knit her fingers with his—as if the contact with his warm flesh would keep her anchored to the here and now.

"You told me about the waves in the restaurant."

"Yes. But I didn't connect it."

"Well, it made me think about some research I'd done. For *Last Train from Eden*."

"Your book where the villain has a nightclub hypnotist act?"

"Yeah. I studied the subject pretty extensively before I started to write. The sound of waves is often used to help induce a trance. Or the subject is asked to imagine himself on a beach, listening to the breakers." With his free hand, Griffon fumbled in his breast pocket and pulled out some folded papers. "So I went back to my library and pulled out some books."

Jessica cringed as she stared at the white sheets.

"This is different from the stuff at dinner," he said quietly. "Something I photocopied this evening. You should read it."

She took the pages and scanned the text—which was from two different books on hypnotism. The material was about how a trance could be induced—often with both a visual and an auditory component. And Griffon was right, the sound of waves was often included. Initially it might take several minutes to put a subject under. But after the person became sensitized to the technique, the process was much easier. Sometimes just a trigger phrase or word was enough.

"Are you saying my mother used hypnotism on me?" she asked when she'd finished reading.

"Tell me about the tape she made."

"When I was eleven or twelve I was having trouble sleeping because—" She stopped abruptly, unwilling to get into how much she'd hated hearing C.R. rant and rave in the evenings when he thought a film wasn't going smoothly. "So my mother made me a tape at our beach house. And…and I used it when I went to bed. There were the waves in the background and her voice talking softly to me, telling me to relax, that I felt wonderful, and that it would be so easy to fall asleep."

"That's a lot like these descriptions of hypnotic inductions." He tapped the sheets.

Jessica nodded. "Mom could have read about it and decided to use it. She liked sneaking things over on people. I guess she got it from dealing with C.R."

"You've hung on to the tape for a long time."

"Yes. After Mom died, I made a collection of things she'd given me. But, really, I haven't used the tape in years. I only thought of it because I was feeling…scared."

He squeezed her hand more tightly. "If someone had searched your apartment, he'd know about the cassette. Or he could have talked to people who lived in your household when you were a kid. Of course, I'm just using the masculine pronoun for convenience. It could just as easily have been a woman. If she knew you were susceptible, all she had to do was push the right buttons to put you into a trance the other morning.''

Jessica shuddered, feeling as if electrodes were worming their way into the tissue of her brain. She remembered the stories her friend Noel Zacharias had told her about what it felt like to have someone messing with your mind. Suddenly it was very hard to breathe. "It happened in the restaurant just with the background music. I got all dreamy and unfocused."

"Partly because you've had a long day, and you were already tired. And partly because the vampire incident was fresh in your subconscious."

Griffon must have seen the horror written on her face because his hand tightened around hers. She closed her eyes and held on to him.

He murmured soothing, reassuring things, and gradually she was able to fight off the panic.

"Did the vampire's voice sound like your mother's?"

"I don't know." She gulped. "But whatever he did worked. What if he tries again?"

Griffon pursed his lips. "Do you remember a movie called *The Ipcress File?* With Michael Caine.

"Yes. Sometimes I remember the films I've seen better than my real life."

He nodded his understanding.

"It was about enemy scientists brainwashing our

agents,'' she continued. ''And there was a noise they used as part of the conditioning.''

''You recall how the Michael Caine character fought it off?''

''By digging something sharp into his palm—so the pain distracted him.''

Griffon lifted her hand and looked at her fingers. ''Well, if you hear waves again, dig your nails into your palms. Hard enough to really hurt. The pain will work for you, too.''

''Are you sure? Or are you just telling me that to make me feel better?''

''Pain is a pretty potent distraction. But nothing's ever for sure. Everything you've taken for granted in your life can change in an instant.''

She raised her eyes to his, silently asking for an explanation, but he got off the couch and went to the window.

Jessica could feel her pulse pounding. ''Tell me what you're thinking.''

It was several seconds before he answered. ''Maybe you're right. Maybe someone was playing vampire the other morning and then they murdered a man and left him in your car, and it has something to do with me. With my books. Not you or your father. When you started filming *Midnight Kiss,* I dragged you into my world. All I have to do is care about someone, and—'' He stopped abruptly. But he'd already revealed so much.

''Thank you for admitting that,'' she breathed.

He gazed at her wearily. ''Don't look so pleased.

I'm a man who can't outrun a curse. And if you get close to me, it will get you, too.''

"That's not true. No one lives under a curse. A curse is no more real than a vampire."

"This isn't getting us anywhere. I live my life the way I have to, and that's all there is to it."

"You're right. We're not going to agree."

"You've had a pretty bad time tonight. You should go to bed. I'll be here if you need me."

"Yes."

She rose off the couch, coming toward him with slow deliberation that belied the wild pounding of her heart. What if he turned away? Yet she gave him every chance to tell her she was making a terrible misjudgment—that when he said he cared, it was only a kind of brotherly affection.

He didn't say anything. He only sighed out a long shaky breath as she stopped a few inches in front of him.

"Jessica."

She knew by the way he said her name that he needed her as much as she needed him. And she was glad because she wanted to wipe away his hurt, his fear of intimacy, in the only way that really counted.

She found his lips with hers. His mouth opened, and when she heard a low animal sound, she didn't know whether it was hers or his.

Could you bind someone with just a kiss? Make them yours? She wanted that. Wanted to seal some kind of agreement. Come to an understanding before he could slip away from her again.

Miraculously it seemed as if he wanted the same

thing. His mouth devoured hers. Lips, tongue, teeth. Sipping, stroking, nipping.

She felt as if she'd left the earth's atmosphere. Weightless, light-headed, starved for oxygen. Starved for Matthew Griffon.

Quickly she grasped his hand and led him down the hall to her bedroom. Frantic to be closer to him, she yanked her shirt over her head. When she looked up, she saw he had done the same thing. He pulled her into his arms, and his hands found the clasp of her bra.

The unwanted garment fell to the floor, and he stood looking at her, caressing her exposed flesh without even touching her. The sensuality alone would have been enough to undo her. But she saw more than that. He was gazing at her as if she were his heart's desire, the thing he longed for most in the world yet knew he could never have.

"God you're so perfect. So beautiful," he murmured.

When he swept her back into his embrace, she arched against him, telling him wordlessly that she needed more.

His lips teased the edge of her ear. "Sweetheart, I may be a little rusty at this, but I think I'm supposed to ask if you have anything we can use."

For a moment his rough whisper confused her.

"Contraceptives."

She looked into his eyes. "I—it's been a long time for me, too."

"Then—"

"But this winter I was dating someone, and I

thought I might—'' She went to her dresser, returning with an unopened package. ''It's just a starter kit.''

''I think it ought to do.''

She set the package on the bedside table. When she turned back to him, he drew her close, his mouth finding hers, his hands stroking down her hips to align her body with his. Feverish sensations burst through her as she felt the hard ridge behind the fly of his jeans. Helplessly caught in the spiraling heat, she surged against his—her body clamoring for closer contact.

Her hand worked its way between them and she found the snap at his waist. As she started to push his jeans down, he took over the job so that she could remove her panties and jeans.

''Ah, Jessie.''

Jessie. Nobody had ever called her that. But then nobody had ever made her feel this trembling need for fulfillment. She clung to him as he brought her down to the bed, tenderly, passionately.

With kisses and caresses, they led each other into a dark, sensual world where every arousing touch, every musky scent, every husky murmur accelerated the beat of some primitive drum inside her body, inside her mind.

''Matthew, come to me,'' she pleaded when the intensity of the pleasure was more than she could bear.

He turned away, and a frisson of fear shot through her. Every other time they'd gotten close, he'd pulled back. Was he doing that now?

When she heard him fumbling with the package on the bedside table, she released the breath that had frozen in her chest.

Then he was over her, looking down into her face with an aching mixture of passion and tenderness as he sank into her secret warmth, joining their bodies into one. He began to move in the ancient rhythm, body to body, soul to soul. Urgent, compelling, building a need between them that clamored for release. She arched against him, once, twice, a dozen times. Higher, faster, harder.

She cried his name as vibrations of ecstasy resonated through every nerve in her body. Seconds later, he was surging into her with his own shuddering climax.

JESSICA KNEW the exact moment when he felt regret. When he was sorry that he'd given in to loving her. But she didn't allow him to pull away. Instead she turned to him and circled him tightly with her arms.

"Don't be dishonest with yourself. Or with me," she whispered. "That was as perfect as it can be for two people."

He didn't speak.

"At least you were honest with your body. Now I guess we'd better take the next step and talk. All the clues to why you're a hermit are in your books, aren't they?"

His jaw tightened.

"I went back to the novel I should have read in the first place. *The Haunting of Greg Matthews.*"

She felt a tremor go through his body. "You read *that* and you still wanted me?"

"It really happened the way you wrote it, didn't it? I mean the beginning. When you begged your parents to take you to the carnival. You were having a wonderful time—until the accident.''

"Yes." The monosyllable was barely audible.

"It *wasn't* your fault. You didn't have anything to do with what happened. It was just horrible luck that the equipment broke, and your parents were in the wrong place at the wrong time.''

Long seconds passed before he answered. "Why don't you quit while you're ahead?''

"Because I care about you. Because I know you care about me. Don't lie about that.''

"That's right. I care. I've been wanting to make love to you for months. I've watched *Appointment in Taos* so many times I can give you a second-by-second description of the love scene. I know you weren't even turned on. You were embarrassed, and I wanted to change the abashed look on your fact to ecstasy. But going to bed with you was a mistake. It can't happen again.''

He rolled away from her, his feet thumping down onto the floor. When he started toward the door, she followed him, heedless of her nakedness—and his. "Watching your parents die like that was a terrible thing to happen to a young, impressionable boy, someone as bright and as sensitive as you. It was bound to affect you in devastating ways.''

A laugh rattled in his throat. "That's a paraphrase of what Grandpa used to say. He spent a bundle on therapy trying to fix me up. And Dr. Winters was good. The best. He made me think I was normal.''

"You are. A normal man. With the normal need to be close to people. To love and be loved. Not just watching home movies of a woman you've never met.''

He stood facing the window, his back rigid. ''Yeah. I may have normal needs, but getting close to me is a death sentence.''

She waited for him to say more—to tell her about Gena. He didn't and she knew she couldn't press him now. She'd made him open up as much as she dared tonight.

''Suppose I said that any time you and I have together would be worth any price I had to pay for it.''

He cursed vehemently, turning and grasping her tightly by the shoulders, holding her at arm's length. ''Don't be a fool.''

''Matthew, I knew before I met you that you were going to be an extraordinary force in my life,'' she insisted urgently. ''Your writing fascinated me and frightened me. You drew me and made me nervous. As a writer and as a man, the person behind the words. Maybe at first it was a kind of challenge—finding out about you when you worked so hard to stay hidden. But it got to be more than that pretty quickly.''

''Why in the hell did you ever have to write that first letter?''

''You believe in destiny. You think you know yours. I think I came into your life to prove that you were wrong about yourself. Or maybe to make everything come out right. Finally.'' She wasn't sure where the speech had come from. It had simply welled up from the depths of her soul. But it felt achingly right. He stood regarding her as if he couldn't quite believe what she had dared to say. Instead of arguing anymore, she reached up, grasping his brawny forearms and tugging. She felt his muscles quiver. Then his arms slowly bent, bringing his body against hers.

When their flesh touched, he let out a shuddering sound that was half sigh, half sob. He clasped her tightly, and they swayed together. His naked body against hers, two people relating on the most primitive of levels.

She wanted to tell him she'd fallen in love with him before they'd met. When they'd only been exchanging heated correspondence about *Midnight Kiss*. She wanted to confess the excuses she'd used to keep the long-distance dialogue going so that she could learn more about him. She wanted to say that she'd be there when he needed her. She knew he couldn't handle that sort of declaration.

"It's late. We both need to get some sleep." Knitting her fingers with his, she led him across the room to the warmth of her bed. She felt the tension ease out of him as he lay beside her. Finally she knew by his regular breathing that he was asleep.

Had she won a victory tonight? Or was he waiting to renew the battle of wills in the morning?

Chapter Eight

The other side of her bed was empty when Jessica awoke a little after seven. For a panicked second she thought Griffon had left the apartment. Then she heard the television set in the living room. Quickly she pulled on a robe, ran a comb through her hair and brushed her teeth. She found Griffon dressed in his jeans and T-shirt from the evening before, sitting on the sofa, his hands wrapped around a mug of coffee.

He must have been listening for Jessica. When he heard her footsteps in the hall, his dark gaze zeroed in on her. For a moment her emotions were unguarded, and the poignant expression of his face made her heart contract.

"Hi," she said, her fingers curling around the tie of the robe. In most situations, she was the one in control. Not with Griffon. "I'm, uh, glad you found my coffee drinkable."

"Barely. I'm going to have to give you lessons." He looked as if he wished he hadn't implied anything even that permanent about their relationship.

"That's good, because I'm not into one-night stands."

"And I'm a little rusty with relationships."

She nodded, desperate to bring the two parts of Matthew Griffon together, the part that longed for a normal life and the part that lived through the books he wrote. He gestured toward the *Morning Sun* spread over the cushions beside him. "Maybe we've lucked out."

"In what regard?"

"So far, last night's death hasn't hit the papers. I guess it was only a big deal to us—and the poor guy who climbed into your car."

"He must have had a mother and father once. People who loved him. Nobody has to end up the way he did when they have people who care about them."

Griffon said nothing. Instead he gave her a long look before getting up and disappearing into the kitchen. When he returned, he was holding out a second mug of coffee.

Jessica accepted it and took a sip. He'd remembered the way she liked it. With milk and sugar.

They both drank in silence until Jessica couldn't stand it any longer. Carefully she set her mug down on the bookshelf. "The important question is, have I lucked out with you, too?" she asked.

"I don't think so."

"I want to talk some more about Greg Matthews."

"I don't."

"Oh, go ahead. Maybe it will be so bad that it will drive me screaming from the room."

He laughed mirthlessly.

Pretending a lot more composure than she felt, she crossed to the sofa and sat down within touching distance. "I didn't exactly have an idyllic childhood, either. I know it can't compare with what happened to you, but it makes me understand the need to escape into your own world where things are better."

"*You* did that?" he whispered.

"Not one specific place." She'd never told anyone about the scenarios she'd made up when she lay awake in bed wishing she'd been born to a father who wasn't obsessed with perfection. Thinking about them had always made her feel weak and vulnerable, but she knew instinctively she had more to gain than lose by sharing her private memories. "I made up a lot of stories in my head at night. My own grade-B productions, I guess you'd call them."

Jessica gave a self-conscious little laugh. "Of course I assigned myself the best parts. The lady doctor who rides into the Western town and saves everyone from a terrible typhoid epidemic—and wins their love and trust. The woman explorer who discovers the diamond mine. The waif who turns out to be the long lost princess. I guess I was wishing I could be those characters instead of C. R. Adams's daughter. Braving floods, fires and enemy warriors would have been easier." For the first time, she saw a glimmer of hope on Matthew's face.

"That bad, huh?" he whispered.

"It's hard to share childhood secrets. But if you can't talk about yourself, talk about Greg," she murmured. "In the book there's a lot of description of his fantasy world. About the evil forces using him as a channel to get at mankind. You made it seem so real. Just like everything you write."

He gave her a direct look. "In a way, it was real. For a little boy who hated reality and made up an elaborate world where he'd rather live."

"Oh, Matthew."

"It didn't start off as an evil place. At first it was like a refuge—a huge forest where there were only animals, no people. Then some of the animals started changing into frightening monsters." He grimaced. "For a couple of years after the carnival, I was on the edge of getting lost there. Dr. Winters dragged me back."

She slid across the space between them, wrapped her arms around him, and held him close like a mother cradling a hurt child. "Tell me all of it. Everything. Every bad thing you've ever been afraid to think or feel."

"You don't want to hear everything. It's better the way I wrote it in the books. With mirrors and sleight of hand to fool you into thinking it's not me."

She let that sink in. "You don't need an artificial barrier between us. Tell me what it was really like."

"Like being powerless. It's much easier making up worlds you can control—like in my books." The phone rang, and he stopped abruptly, as if relieved that he didn't have to reveal any more of his memories.

Exasperated at the interruption, Jessica reached for the receiver.

"Hello?"

"Jessica."

It was Dan Cassidy, an assistant state's attorney who happened to be married to Sabrina Barkley—the friend who'd suggested the *Midnight Kiss* project to her last year.

"Yes?"

"I'm calling about the man you found in your car last night."

She gulped and sat up straighter, knowing from the sound of Dan's voice that he wasn't calling with good news. Griffon was watching her, his face tense, and she reached to grip his hand with her free one.

"He was murdered," her friend said.

"Oh, no."

"They did the autopsy first thing this morning, so I've got the preliminaries." Dan paused. "I see from the police report that you say you never met him."

"Dan, I didn't." She choked around the lump that had formed in her windpipe.

"What's wrong?" Griffon asked urgently, moving so that his ear was near the one she had pressed against the receiver.

"The medical examiner's office has never seen a case like this. It's pretty wild. Apparently he was exsanguinated."

"Exsanguinated?"

Beside her Griffon sucked in a startled breath.

Dan continued, "Yeah. He died from having the blood drained out of his body. Through those two holes in his neck."

Jessica's knuckles whitened around the receiver as she tried to listen to the rest of Dan's conversation.

"I'll let you know if there are any new developments, and I might need to question you again and possibly the rest of the film crew, too."

"Can we keep this out of the papers?" she asked.

"I don't know. But I'll see if I can restrict the autopsy report."

When she'd hung up, her whole body was shaking. She turned frightened eyes to the man beside her, searching for answers and reassurance. But his features were tightly drawn.

"Hold me."

Griffon held her until the tremors stopped.

"You said vampires don't exist," she whispered against his chest.

"They only live in the world of fiction and superstition. But someone is going to a lot of trouble to make them *look* real. And the sooner we find out who and why, the better."

GRIFFON DROVE Jessica to 43 Light Street for the day's rehearsal. "Do you think I can get away without telling the cast about the murder?" she asked. "We've got so much to do, and I know that everyone's going to be upset."

"I'd come clean with them."

"I guess you're right," Jessica admitted. "But I'd like to get through one more day before I drop the bombshell. I'll tell them at five. Maybe they'll be too worn-out to go into hysterics."

Griffon sighed. "That might work, but you'd better talk to Reva this morning, so she'll have an official response ready if we have to make a statement to the media."

"Okay."

Griffon didn't ask if she wanted him to stay with

her. He just came along—as if he knew how much she needed him and was willing to let the rest of their problems go for the time being.

He opened up the rehearsal room while she went on to her office. When she heard a man's voice inside, she stopped short. Then she realized it was Perry. Who was in there with him? The police? She peeked apprehensively through the door and saw he was on the phone.

"Listen, John, if you've got something better I'm sure I can get out of my—" He broke off abruptly and hung up the receiver when he spotted Jessica.

"Agents! They'll drive you crazy." Looking like a little boy who'd been caught stealing apples, he rushed past her.

She was too relieved to find out he was alone to analyze what he'd been saying—or to ask if he'd been calling New York on her nickel.

"Perry, wait!" she called out.

The actor paused. "Yeah?"

"Let the cast know we'll start fifteen minutes late— about 10:15, and if you see Reva around, tell her I need to talk to her right away."

"Sure thing."

He must have caught up to her assistant down the hall, because a few minutes later Reva popped into the office. "Perry said you were looking for me?"

"Yes, something's come up that you need to know about."

Matthew filed in after Reva and closed the door. As he leaned casually against the wall, Jessica suddenly suspected at least one of the reasons why he'd come up here with her. He wanted to see Reva's reaction when she heard about the murder.

Jessica motioned her assistant into the seat in front of the desk.

"A man was found dead in my car in the parking garage last night," she began.

"What?" Reva gasped, her eyes widening.

Trying to keep the emotion out of her voice, Jessica filled the woman in on the strange death and the possible adverse publicity the incident might generate.

"The others aren't going to like this," the redhead predicted. "I don't like it much myself." Vigorously she rubbed at the goose bumps on her arm.

"No one in his right mind would like it," Jessica murmured. "So please keep everything I've told you strictly confidential."

"I'll try. But you know how rumors buzz around here."

JESSICA TOOK a deep breath and called the rehearsal meeting to order. No matter what, she couldn't afford to have this production fall apart. Not only had she invested everything she'd saved, but she had her backers' interest to think of, too. And that included Matthew's.

The cast was gathered around the table obviously unaware that anything unusual had happened the night before. Or maybe one of them was acting. Her appraising gaze swept each individual. Perry was finishing up a package of vending machine doughnuts and sipping a soda. The sight of that breakfast combination made Jessica's stomach turn over. Edward must have had a bad night, too, because he was wearing dark tinted glasses. God, she hoped he wasn't drinking again. Diedre and Heather seemed to have been arguing when she'd come in, but they'd stopped and were now sitting next to each other as if nothing had happened. Perhaps they'd been practicing their mother/daughter conflict.

Surprisingly, for the next two hours, the reading went smoothly. Edward and Diedre had learned all their lines, and Perry's interpretation of the vampire was right on target. Only Heather seemed a bit unsure of herself—but that was to be expected with her age and limited experience.

They had reached the last scene when a sudden commotion in the hall made Diedre stop in midsentence.

"You can't go in there!"

"Who's going to stop me?"

The door burst open and a burly man with short-cropped blond hair and a bulldog chin plowed into room. He was followed by a distraught Reva Kane.

Before Jessica could get out of her seat, Griffon sprang from his chair in the corner and laid a restraining grasp of the intruder's shoulder. "Who the hell are you?"

"I'm Garrison Montgomery, from the *Baltimore Sun,* and I'm here to find out what you people know about last night's vampire murder." He twisted out of Griffon's grip and took a step back.

There were gasps around the room, and Jessica felt her heart sink. She should have taken Matthew's advice and told the cast right away.

"I don't know a damn thing!" Perry denied quickly. His gaze shot to Jessica. "Do you?"

"I—"

Thankfully, Matthew took over for her. "Late last night, a man was found dead in Jessica's car. But as far as we know, the murder had nothing to do with her, anyone in the cast, or the movie," he assured everybody.

"That's not what they were saying down at the morgue. They've got a stiff in the freezer with all the blood drained out of his body, and somebody thinks it might've been done as a vampire movie publicity stunt."

Diedre and Edward gasped again.

"Oh, yuck," Heather exclaimed.

Perry leaned forward. "Hey, a real life vampire right here in Charm City. Maybe if they catch him, I can pick up some pointers."

"Grow up, Dunmore," Diedre admonished. "This is serious." Then she turned to the head of the table. "You really should have told us about this."

Jessica accepted the scolding. "You're right. But there wasn't much information to share. I'm sure the police will find out what actually happened." She turned to the reporter. "That's all I have to say on the subject so if you'll kindly leave, we can get back to our rehearsal."

But the man didn't budge. "I want some background from your vampire expert—the guy that writes all those horror stories."

"Say the word and I'll toss him," Matthew offered.

For a moment, Jessica's eyes flashed to his. She

didn't doubt he would do it. But the relief would only be temporary. She remembered how Montgomery had hounded her friend Erin after she'd been abducted last Christmas. She hadn't talked to him, but he'd written a nasty little piece anyway. And she was sure he was going to do a vampire article whether they cooperated or not.

"This is Matthew Griffon," she said, "and if he's willing to answer a few questions, then I guess I have no objections. You might as well do it in here so everyone can find out what's going to be in tomorrow's paper."

Griffon nodded, but the tight line of his chin showed he wasn't happy about the interview. However, the reporter was already pulling up a chair and digging into his coat pocket for a notebook and pen.

"So when did all this vampire stuff get started?" he asked.

"It's a persistent legend in human history going back as far as the ancient Greeks, the early Babylonians, and the Chinese. Vampires were used to explain everything from sudden deaths to crop failures. As late as 1910, New Englanders were still occasionally digging up graves and performing rites to make sure family members stayed dead."

As Matthew talked about the vampire's supernatural abilities to turn into cats, bats, mice and butterflies, Jessica was impressed by how easily he slipped into the role of professor. Obviously he'd done years of research.

The cast, hesitatingly at first, and then with more assertiveness, pushed him for details on how to spot a vampire and stop one in his tracks. Only Reva, who sat with her fingers clenched in her lap, and Heather who seemed almost hypnotized by Matthew's voice, didn't speak up.

Montgomery was still searching for an angle for his story. "So what makes these vampire books and movies such hits?"

"They appeal to our fear and fascination with the dark side of life. Death. Obsession. Uncontrollable desire." Griffon's eyes flicked to Jessica's, then away.

She cleared her throat. "I think that's enough. Thank you, Mr. Griffon."

"Just a word of caution," he added to the reporter. "Be very careful what you write. Don't tie this to real life. Anything that smacks of the occult can make people panic. Vigilante groups. Vampire hunts. Reputations shattered. Innocent people could get hurt."

"You're a fine one to talk," Montgomery shot back. "Your books are as scary as they come."

"But there's a world of difference between reading a novel about the supernatural and seeing a headline, 'Vampire Murder,' across the front page of the Baltimore paper."

Montgomery got up to leave. "This isn't the *Inquirer,* but no matter how I play it, I'm sure you're going to have a lot more interest as soon as this one hits the wire."

As he lumbered out, the professional demeanor of the cast cracked like a dam after a twenty-inch rainfall.

"The press will jolly well be all over us," Edward complained. "Digging into our lives, dissecting every fault in full public view." He shuddered.

Diedre reached over and patted his hand. "I know how you feel." Jessica recalled Matthew's dossier on Diedre, and the custody battle she'd endured.

Perry's expression was thoughtful. Then, as if he'd slipped into another character, his mouth turned down into a scowl. "I don't want any trouble with the press. And I don't have to stick around this two-bit film and watch my career turned into confetti." He started to rise, but Griffon pushed him back into his seat.

Jessica jumped in before anyone could escalate the anxiety level. "None of you has been affected by this yet. And you won't be. As long as the press can't find us."

"All they have to do is check the phone book," Perry snapped.

"Not if we push up the schedule a few days early and all move out to the Carmichael house for rehearsals. Nobody knows we rented the place, and the town won't be aware that anything's going on unless somebody happens to spot the film crew next week. We're working entirely on private property, so it's not like we're stopping traffic in downtown Hampstead while we film a scene at the café," Jessica replied.

There were grumbles around the table about the inconvenience of living at the estate.

"I'll add two hundred dollars a day bonus and take care of all your living expenses," Griffon offered.

Jessica shot him a startled look. That offer would cost him an extra twenty thousand at least. But he seemed willing to make the concessions, and the cast grudgingly accepted the move. Since it was unlikely they'd get any more work done, she called it quits for the day. Everyone was supposed to be out in Hampstead by four o'clock the next day.

Reva hung back after the actors had left. "I let you down with that nut of a reporter. I should have been able to keep him from disrupting your meeting. And about yesterday. I really didn't mean to eavesdrop," she apologized.

"I don't think anything short of dynamite could have stopped Mr. Montgomery," Jessica said wryly.

"Well, anyway. I'd like to apologize by doing some extra work—like supervising the cleaning of the mansion and making sure the beds have fresh linens. And I can have a catering service provide lunch and dinner for the first few days, and get groceries for breakfast and snacks."

"That would be wonderful. Thank you." Jessica flashed her an appreciative smile.

AFTER A HECTIC twenty-four hours of making arrangements, Jessica was on her way out to Hampstead again. It had been raining all day, a pounding downpour that challenged her windshield wipers to a highspeed duel and won. Matthew was supposed to meet her at the site—or at least that was the message he'd left on her answering machine last night.

Except for a brief exchange after yesterday's meeting, they hadn't spoken. She knew he was avoiding her. Was he mad at her for sacrificing him to that reporter? Or was he wishing they hadn't gotten so close the night before? She wanted to hear his reassurances, but she was afraid to ask.

Montgomery's article had run in the Feature Section, not on the front page. A few details of the murder were covered in the first paragraph but the thrust of the piece was getting an exclusive interview with the reclusive Matthew Griffon. There was even a quote from his publisher about his last book selling over five million copies and his new three-book contract for nearly twelve million dollars. No wonder the man could afford to pay the cast an incentive bonus.

Jessica's car was packed to the limit, and she could feel every bounce as she headed up the access road to the estate. The dirt and gravel driveway was awash in mud, and she had to go slowly. Crossing the wood bridge over the river, she was shocked at how much the water had risen in just a few days. It was mere inches below the wooden planks she was rumbling over—which did nothing for her sense of security. And when she finally pulled up in front of the mansion, memories of her first spooky visit made her stomach clench. Hands wrapped around the wheel, she sat staring at the house through the steadily falling rain. Yesterday, she'd thought of this place as a refuge where they'd be safe from the prying eyes of the press. But what if something more sinister was waiting for them here? Shaking away the morbid thoughts, she opened the car door and dashed for the porch.

At least this time the lights were all on, and Reva came bustling out of the kitchen with a smile on her face.

"Lovely spring weather," Jessica said, shaking off wet droplets from her hair.

"If it keeps up, you'll have to change the garden argument to a mud fight."

Jessica laughed. "I'm sure Diedre would love that. Have you been here long?"

"Three or four hours. I've finished up with the cleaning crew. The caterers stocked the kitchen and left prepared meals for tonight and tomorrow in the refrigerator. Now all we have to do is wait for the cast to arrive."

"Great." Jessica strove to sound enthusiastic. "I've got to get the rest of the stuff from my car."

"I'll help you bring it in."

A few minutes later, Reva came back carrying a heavy box Jessica hadn't been able to lift by herself.

"Here, let me help you with that one—it weighs a ton," she offered, setting down her suitcase.

"No, I'm fine," Reva said as she lowered the crate to the floor.

"You must be in better shape than I am."

"Well, I work out a couple of times a week," she said dismissively.

When they'd finished unloading, Jessica claimed the master bedroom with its private, if somewhat antiquated, bath as her own. As she looked out the window, Matthew's trailer pulled up only a few dozen yards from the house. She waited eagerly for him to get out, but he didn't appear. With a sigh she began to unpack.

By the time she had changed into a dry outfit and hung up her clothes, she could hear voices downstairs. Walking to her door, she listened quietly. First she detected Perry. Then Diedre. As each new arrival joined the conversation, she waited to hear Griffon's voice. When he didn't join the group, she closed her door and sat down heavily on the bed. Briefly she thought about going out to the trailer. Then she shook her head. She was damned if she was going to let Matthew see how insecure she was feeling.

GRIFFON DIDN'T SHOW UP until they were all sitting around the dining room table, passing plates of lasagna and salads left by the catering service. Acknowledging the group with a nod, he slipped into the empty chair across from Jessica.

"Some woman reporter was pounding on my door at two in the morning," Perry complained.

"How did you manage to get rid of her?" Edward asked dryly.

"I asked her what her blood type was."

Griffon and Vanesco laughed. Diedre was less amused. "I guess that will be spread across tomorrow's paper, too. I wasn't thrilled with what I read this morning."

"By the way, how is everybody's room?" Jessica changed the subject.

Diedre shrugged. "It's not the Ritz, but I've stayed in worse."

"How come *she* got the big room with the canopy bed and I got stuck in a closet with a cot?" Heather whined.

"It's all a matter of experience and timing, my dear," the older actress confided.

"What she means is that she got here on time and you were a half hour late," Reva translated.

The bickering and jibes grated on Jessica's nerves. It reminded her too much of her childhood and the shallow, self-centered people who thought they could gain something by pretending to be friendly with her father. She glanced up and found Matthew studying her. What was he thinking? But his eyes gave nothing away. Well, she'd had enough of not knowing where she stood with him. They'd talk later—when they didn't have an audience.

After dinner, while she went over the next day's schedule with the cast, he silently left the table. The front door opened and closed, and she knew he was heading back to his trailer.

Most of the cast members had moved into the den and were arguing about what to watch on the TV. From the high volume and rock soundtrack, it seemed the younger generation was prevailing.

Tension compressed Jessica's chest as she picked up her jacket and headed toward the trailer. The rain was still pounding down, and as she stepped out into the night, a bolt of lightning jagged menacingly across the sky. She hoped it wasn't a bad omen.

Chapter Nine

Griffon answered her knock so quickly that Jessica wondered if he'd been watching out the window as she'd crossed the parking area.

"That was fast!"

"I knew it would be you, and I don't want you standing out in the rain."

Her spirits leapt—just a little. At least he cared about her welfare. Yet his guarded expression made her heart start to pound as she stepped into the familiar room. If this was going to be a painful confrontation, she'd get it over with as quickly as possible. But she wasn't going to walk away empty-handed. "You've been avoiding me."

"I said you were perceptive."

"You don't want to finish the discussion Dan's call interrupted."

He folded his hands across his chest. "That's right."

"Avoidance isn't a very constructive way to deal with problems."

"Where'd you get that—from Oprah?"

"It's something I've had to deal with in my own life."

"Good for you!"

Unwilling to let him see how shaky she really was, Jessica dropped onto the sofa. Griffon propped his hips against the desk.

"Tell me about the rest of the bad things that happened to you."

His jaw was rigid, his eyes defiant. "What gives *you* the right to ask me that?"

The words she'd intended to hold back slipped out. "I love you." Anxiously she watched his face. She wasn't sure what she expected. Certainly not the flash of pain he struggled to hide. "And—and I think you feel something for me," she whispered. "But if you tell me you don't care, I'll get up and walk out of here."

Her heart blocked her windpipe. Seconds ticked by, but he said nothing.

"Matthew," she said softly, "we developed a pretty intense relationship before we ever laid eyes on each other. Then we met, and—"

"You were frightened of me." He bit off the words.

"Yes. Because you made sure I would be—as a way of keeping me from getting any closer."

His lips were pressed so tightly that they looked as though they'd never open again. But she wasn't going to let him stonewall. "But when terrible, disturbing things started happening to me, you were there every time I needed you."

"I'm not going to run out on you when you're in trouble. Not when you're filming my book."

"And after we finish filming? Then are you going to just walk away from us?"

He didn't answer.

She added more fuel to the fire. "A man doesn't make love the way you did the other night unless he cares deeply about his partner."

He looked as if she'd knocked the breath out of him. "Yes, I care," he rasped. "That's why I'm trying to protect you. So stop pushing me, dammit!"

"Give me some facts. Let me be the judge of whether I need protecting."

His eyes turned flinty. "Okay, do you want to hear about Matthew Griffon the murderer? Or Matthew Griffon the drug addict?"

The tension in his body was like heat lightning crackling between them. "You're not a murderer. And you're not a drug addict."

"Right. I've been off drugs for the past six years. And it's eight years since I killed the woman I loved," he flung at her.

"Stop it!"

"It happened because I needed her too much. Or that's the way it started. With *my* needs. We met in college. In the first semester of Seventeenth Century English Poetry." He spoke quickly, the raw anguish in his voice making her vision blur. "We were both juniors. But I was a year older than Gwen, because I couldn't keep up with my class after the carnival. Being with her was like a fantasy come true. She was smart and funny and pretty. Popular. With lots of friends. And she was attracted to *me*. I fell head over heels in love with her, *needed* to be in love with her.

Grandpa had died, and I was lonely. If I hadn't fixed on her, it would have been one of the other girls in my class.''

Jessica scrambled off the sofa and went to him, taking him by the forearms. ''Do you always cast your motives in the worst possible light? A lot of kids in college are looking for a relationship. It's the age when young adults pair up.''

He plowed on, as if determined to get it over with now that he'd started. ''Grandpa left me some money, so I didn't have to worry about supporting her. We got married before senior year and moved into a little apartment in Boston near the university. Then I started graduate school in English. But I'd begun selling some short stories to the fantasy magazines, and I knew that's what I really wanted to do. So I decided to drop out of the Ph.D. program.''

''Gwen didn't agree?'' Jessica asked.

He shook his head. ''We were on the way back to Boston after spring break, and we were having one of our fights about my wanting to spend full-time writing genre fiction when I had a brilliant academic career ahead of me. It was all we seemed to talk about. She thought anyone who pandered to the popular market had sold out. I kept reminding her that everyone from Shakespeare to Wordsworth to Dickinson had written for the people. We—'' He stopped abruptly and gulped in a lungful of air. ''Anyway I'd hurt my hand wind sailing, so she was driving. It was raining pretty hard, and I shouldn't have been distracting her. She…she skidded on a curve and went down an embankment.''

Jessica held him fiercely. "Matthew, it was an *accident!* Her accident. You weren't even in the driver's seat."

He kept talking, as if she hadn't said anything, his voice strangled. "The car landed on its side. She was trying to get out of the car through the passenger door when the gas tank exploded. I was thrown clear. It seemed like I broke just about every bone in my body. Plus there were a lot of internal injuries."

As Jessica tried to imagine that kind of damage, her mind made an intuitive leap. "You were in terrible pain. That's why they had to put you on drugs."

"Yeah. I needed to stay doped up. But not just for the physical stuff. I wanted to forget I'd never see Gwen again. And forget the police interrogation. They had a hard time believing she'd been driving, since they found her in the passenger's seat. Sometimes I wonder if I made that part up."

"Matthew. Matthew." She held him, rocked him, felt him shaking in her arms as he finally lost the battle for emotional control.

"I didn't want to live. I don't know why I did."

"So you could write *Midnight Kiss* and all the other wonderful books that people love."

He snorted. "I write mass market fiction. Stuff that will be forgotten in fifty years."

"No! You write sensitive, evocative stories that have won a lot of critical acclaim. But that's not the issue. The point is you lost three people you loved very much. Three people you needed in your life. It's natural—"

"Oh, please! You think *Midnight Kiss* is a wonderfully evocative tale about a vampire? Where the hell do you think I learned what it feels like to want something, to crave something so much that your life revolves around getting it—and at the same time you know it is going to kill you? From being hooked on morphine.''

She pressed him closer, as if her slender body could shelter him from all the anguish he'd stored up during the long, lonely years when he'd withdrawn from the world. ''I didn't know that's what you were writing about. I can understand it now. But you're no different from any other great writer. They all use their own lives. And if you're worried about translating drugs into art, think about Coleridge or William Burroughs or Aldous Huxley or the Beatles, for that matter. In your case, you've transmuted your pain into something that gives your readers a very powerful experience.''

The anguished look in his eyes was the one she'd seen when she said she loved him.

''How do you think I know the soul of the vampire?'' he continued. ''The destroyer. He has a driving need to get close to people. He feeds on them, even though he knows it will end in their death.''

''Stop it! Stop! You don't feed on anyone. What happened to you at the carnival and with Gwen was bad luck. Terrible luck. You didn't cause it. Every kid alive wheedles what he wants from his parents. Yours were just in the wrong place at the wrong time. And later, with Gwen, you weren't even driving the car. How can you believe it was your fault?''

He tried to pull away from her. She wouldn't let him go as she spoke urgently, rapidly. ''When I first read your work, I knew you called to something deep in my soul. In a way, that frightened me, because your work was so real—so universally true. So close to the secrets everybody hides. Damn you, Matthew Griffon. You're not as unique as you think. You have the same fears and the same need to love and be loved as everyone else. It's just that every time you've reached out to people, fate has slapped you in the face.''

She could see he was listening to her. Really listening. Knowing that she might never get another chance, she went on, her voice breaking up around the edges. ''Matthew, you're a heck of a lot more articulate than most people, but it wasn't just your writing that drew me. I had to know the man who plucked at so many of the chords playing in my head. That was why I came up with the idea of turning one of your books into a movie. In a way, it was just an excuse to correspond with you, to meet you. So stop trying to protect me. I worked hard to get you into my life. I'm not going to give you up.''

He looked lost and helpless, as if the lifeline he'd clung to for so many years had unraveled in his fingers, and there was no way to weave it back together. Aching to replace the tattered threads with something more substantial, she leaned forward and pressed her lips softly to his. ''This time it's going to be different,'' she whispered.

He went completely still, and she felt her heart lurch as she sensed her life hanging in the balance. Death would be easier than rejection. But she could say nothing else, do nothing else except offer her love to him.

Eternity stretched before her as she sensed the struggle inside him. ''I can't...'' he groaned, and the world crumbled away from under her.

In the next moment, his mouth opened against hers and she knew she'd misunderstood the intent of his words. He couldn't turn away from her. Not now, anyway.

''Yes,'' she whispered, her breath mingling with his. ''Take anything you want. And give me what I need.''

His arms shook as he scooped her up, cradling her against his length. He kissed her hungrily, greedily, taking and giving, just as she had asked. Frantic hands tugged at clothing—his and hers.

They both gasped as hot naked flesh melded together. Then their hands began to move over each others' bodies, finding exquisitely sensitive places. Ripples of pleasure swept across her skin like fire across a tinder-dry landscape.

Thankfully the last thing she'd done before she'd left her apartment was stuff the box of condoms into her purse. Now she retrieved it on the way to the bedroom.

''When you stayed here, I lay awake most of the night thinking about climbing into bed with you and taking you into my arms,'' he whispered huskily.

''Maybe because I was silently calling you.'' Her hand entwined with his, she climbed onto the wide bunk.

''Jessie. Jessie.'' He came down beside her, cradling the length of her body against his—kissing her, touching her, loving her with a heart-stopping mixture of passion and tenderness. "Tell me this isn't one of my fantasies."

"It's as real as anything in heaven or earth," she murmured. But the fevered words were only a pale echo of what she was feeling. Emotionally. Physically. Her heart swelled with love for Matthew. She wanted only to give and give to him. And the gift came back to her as swift, intense pleasure flooding through her being. With little cries, she twisted against him, aching for their ultimate joining.

He growled something low and possessive. Then he was inside her, moving, demanding, driving her to heights she'd thought were impossible until the first time they'd made love.

Afterward for golden minutes, she cuddled against him, basking in satisfaction and the triumph of proving to him once again that they belonged together.

He kissed her softly on the temple and held her close. But she sensed a tension in him that shouldn't be there.

"Matthew?"

"Jessica, I'm not going to lie to you. I'm afraid for you."

"I'm not. Not about us. We're good together. Not bad."

"I wish I had your confidence."

She sighed. "I wish I didn't have to go back to the mansion. But tongues are going to wag if I spend the night here."

He laughed softly. "You're so direct with me. Do you care about them?"

"I wouldn't—except that the cast doesn't need another distraction right now."

His arms circled around her. "Now that you're here, I want you in my bed a little while longer."

"I think we're going to have to make a trip into town to replace my starter kit," she murmured, her naked toes playing with the hair on his shin.

He looked suddenly uncertain. "Jessica, I'm not used to indulging myself like this."

"Well, I'll give you permission to be as selfish as you want."

"Oh, yeah?" He rolled her to her back and kissed her hungrily.

IT WAS MORE than an hour later when Jessica finally said a lingering good-night to Griffon and closed the door of the camper. The rain was coming down in sheets now, making it hard to see more than a few feet in front of her face. As she dashed across the muddy ground to the mansion, she was thankful for the dim glow of the porch light to guide her.

Rain lashed her through the screen as she maneuvered carefully across the slippery boards of the porch. The television set was blaring from the den, so she knew some of the others were still awake. What were her chances of slipping upstairs and into her room without anyone knowing how long she'd been gone?

She was halfway across the slick floor when the light flicked off, plunging her into near total darkness.

"Is somebody there?" she called out, standing very still.

The only answer was a strange *whoop, whoop,*

whooping sound that sent a shiver from the base of her spine all the way up into her hair.

"Wh-who's that?" she called out again.

In the next moment, a terrifying black shape swooped down on her like a demon out of hell. She screamed and ducked.

Whoop, whoop, whoop.

It flapped past her face, brushing her neck.

"Help! Matthew, someone please help me!"

No one heard above the noise of the television. In a panic she stumbled across the porch, slipped and then bumped into a chair that was only a dark shape in her path. With her pulse drumming in her ears, she reached the wall, holding on tight with one hand and feeling for the door with the other.

Relief surged through her—until she turned the knob and found it locked.

Whoop, whoop, whoop.

As if it knew it had her trapped, the creature swooped at her again.

Chapter Ten

Lowering her head and moaning softly, Jessica tried to protect her neck as the wings flapped around her in the darkness.

Her mind was functioning on a very primitive level. "The vampire," she sobbed. "The vampire."

It had sucked the life from the man in her car. It had followed them here, and now it was after *her*.

Hands clenched into fists, she pounded on the door. No one came. She could barely see what she was doing, and she wasn't sure whether she could make it back across the slippery expanse of the porch before the creature got her.

Desperately she twisted this way and that in the darkness, her hands scrabbled for a defensive weapon. She felt the back of a sofa, a shelf, a chair. Finally her fingers curled around the top of a wicker plant stand.

With a cry of relief, she stooped down and snatched at the wooden base, hurling a clay flowerpot into the air as she swung the planter up like a baseball bat. The pot broke apart as it hit the floor, but Jessica hardly registered the resounding crash or the rain and wind lashing at her through the screen. She was too intent on wielding her newfound weapon. Her adrenaline was pumping, and anger had transformed her terror into defiance. Her hands wrapped firmly around the shaft of the stand, she braced her hips against the wall and flailed with manic energy, cutting through the air with a high, whistling sound.

The edge of the planter bounced against the board along the top of the screen and clanged off a light fixture. But the collisions were only minor distractions. Her goal was to destroy the thing that had come out of the darkness to assault her.

She gave a shout of triumph as the makeshift bludgeon smacked into something with a different texture from the architectural elements she'd been blindly assaulting. This time she'd struck flesh and blood. The creature squealed, and she heard it thump onto the floor. At the same time she realized that someone else was on the porch.

"Jessica!"

It was Griffon, and he was running toward her, shouting her name. He smacked into the same chair she'd hit, cursed and tossed the solid piece of furniture out of the way as if it were a sofa cushion.

He reached her, turning her toward him, his hands digging into her shoulders. "Jessie, what's wrong? Are you all right?"

"The vampire," she gasped. "It came after me." The weapon slipped from her fingers, and she pointed in the direction where she thought the creature had fallen.

Griffon switched on a flashlight, playing the beam back and forth across the floor. When the light illuminated the shattered remains of the flowerpot, he paused.

"That?"

"No! Something alive—with wings. Something going 'whoop, whoop, whoop' and flapping around my head like it was going to bite me on the neck."

He began to search again. Jessica gave a strangled gasp when the beam hit a crumpled little body that had fallen behind a wicker rocker. The thing was black and evil looking.

"I think it's a bat." Griffon moved the chair out of the way and knelt. Jessica grasped his forearm, trying to pull him back, as if the creature were going to spring at him like Dracula from his coffin.

"Keep away from it!"

"It's just a bat," he repeated, poking the lifeless body with a shard from the planter. Yet she sensed something in his reaction that he wasn't sharing.

Jessica stared at the grotesque little visage and the membranous wings that spread limply across the floor. "God, it looks like a gargoyle. Or worse."

"I know. They're ugly as sin. But it was probably as frightened of you as you were of it. Bats sleep during the day and go out to feed at night. I guess it must have gotten trapped on the porch. Or maybe the screen is torn."

"In *Midnight Kiss,* the vampire came to her as a bat!"

"Jessica, that's fiction," he repeated the assurance he'd given her several times before. "Fiction and reality are different."

"You said your books reflected reality. Only it was disguised."

"That wasn't what I meant," he said tightly.

She wished that she could see his expression better, but the light was too dim. "It came after me," she repeated in a low voice.

Griffon closed the distance between them and held her tight. "It was in my hair," she whispered, struggling to keep her voice steady. "And my face. And...and...when I tried to get away, the door was locked."

"Which door?" he asked sharply.

"To the kitchen. I wasn't sure I could cross the porch again before it got me." She glanced toward the corpse on the floor this time seeing it for what it was—an animal she had killed. "I—I went after that poor little thing like a madwoman."

"You have plenty of reasons to be jumpy after what's been happening. Don't blame yourself."

"Don't blame yourself for what?" another voice asked. "What's happened?"

They turned to find Reva standing in the doorway looking worried. Behind her hovered a pale and uncertain Heather Nielson.

"A bat was out here," Griffon explained matter-of-factly, pointing toward the creature. "It flew into Jessica's hair and frightened her. She whacked it with a plant stand."

"Oh, yuck!" Heather wrinkled her pretty nose as she stole a look at the dead animal.

Reva gave a little shiver.

"Let's go inside," Griffon steered Jessica toward the door. Reva fell back as he advanced.

Feeling weary and helpless, Jessica stood in the middle of the kitchen with her arms wrapped around her shoulders. "Didn't anyone hear me banging around out there?" she asked.

"How could they, with Perry's dumb war movie on TV?" Heather asked. "I only heard something when I came in to the kitchen to get a diet soda." She turned to Reva. "I can't find any! Did you forget to buy it?"

"Diet soda! That's the last thing I was thinking about," the secretary muttered.

"How did you know we were out on the porch?" Griffon questioned.

"I was going to do some work at the kitchen table," Reva answered, pointing to the pile of papers lying in one corner. "The light's not good enough in the library."

"Was the door locked when you came out onto the porch?" Griffon asked.

Reva hesitated for a fraction of a second. "Yes."

"It was unlocked when I left the house," Jessica interjected.

"Well, you've been gone for hours, so anybody could have bolted it," her secretary said peevishly. "We're out in the middle of nowhere, you know. You don't want uninvited company to wander in."

Griffon nodded and crossed to the kitchen table where he took several paper napkins from the stack in the holder. Then he started opening cabinets until he found the plastic grocery bags Reva had put away.

"What are you going to do?" she asked as he retraced his steps toward the door.

"Wrap up the bat. I want it checked out by a lab."

Jessica felt her chest constrict. "For what? You said—I mean, if it's really just…"

"Just what?" Heather interjected, her voice rising to a squeak.

Jessica shook her head, looking at the young actress's pinched features and wishing she'd kept her mouth shut. All she needed was to get the cast in a panic.

"Bats can carry rabies," Griffon answered the previous question. "It didn't break your skin or anything, did it?"

Jessica ran her hands over her face and arms, and before she could stop herself, she delicately probed the skin of her neck where she'd seen the marks on the dead man two nights before. When she realized everyone was watching her, she flushed. "I don't think so."

Heather wrenched her gaze away from Jessica and focused on the napkins as if Griffon were holding a fistful of green slime. "I'm going home!"

"In this rain?" Jessica asked, wondering if she'd heard correctly.

"Yes. I'm getting out of this damn freak show. I don't care how much extra you're willing to pay. I didn't sign a contract saying I was going to stay in a haunted house with bats flying around, and I've had enough."

"Too bad I didn't insist on a written agreement," Griffon shot back.

"We're not in a prison, and you're not the warden."

"Are you coming back for the morning rehearsal?" Reva asked.

"No." Her face set in a defiant mask, Heather turned on her heels and started for the stairs. Reva trailed after her. Jessica was left standing in the middle of the kitchen with Griffon. She looked at him bleakly.

"Heather can be replaced," he said. "You'll get your movie made. One way or the other."

She couldn't summon the energy to agree.

Griffon must have sensed that if he touched her, she would shatter. Instead he took the bag and napkins back outside. When he didn't reappear, Jessica assumed he'd taken the little body to the trailer.

Too wrung out to stand any longer, she sank onto one of the kitchen chairs. What was going to go wrong next? She had just rested her head in her hands when she heard footsteps on the stairs and forced herself to sit up straight. Heather came into the kitchen with a duffel slung over one shoulder and a hanging bag over the other. "Lucky I didn't unpack," she muttered.

"Heather, won't you reconsider?"

"This place is jinxed. This whole production is jinxed."

"Has something happened to *you?*"

"Forget it."

"Heather, please."

The young actress shook her head tightly and sailed onto the porch. A minute later, a car engine started, then wheels spun in the wet gravel.

Jessica wanted to weep. Yet she held back the tears. It would be comforting to think the bat on the porch was only bad luck. More likely somebody had put it there and locked the door so she'd be trapped with the creature when she came back from the trailer. And why not? Everything else, including the dead man in her car, looked like someone was trying to make sure *Midnight Kiss* was never filmed.

She sighed. Griffon had been right all along. She should have been looking for suspects. And motives. It was hard to believe all this really had anything to do with her father. But what, then?

Cupping her chin in her hands, she tried to consider each of the people involved in the project. Heather. Well, she'd just about proven it wasn't her, unless she was staging this defection for effect. Or was that a master stroke in the girl's plot? To wait until the worst possible moment to leave?

Jessica's head began to pound. Did she really think dim little Heather had somehow sucked all the blood out of a vagrant, dragged him past the security guard and put him into her car in the Scarlet House garage? Not unless she'd had help.

As Jessica considered that possibility, her mind leaped to a conversation she'd only half heard because she had been focused on other things. Two days ago when she and Griffon had come down to the office, Perry had been talking on the phone to his agent. What had he said? Something about a better offer and getting out of—? His contract? Was that why he'd looked so guilty and slammed down the phone?

And what if it were true? That didn't make him a murderer?

She didn't know. She didn't know how to cope with this by herself. But there was one thing she was sure of. She needed to find Griffon. To share this with him, and most of all to just be with him.

As she stepped out onto the porch again, she braced herself for a black shape to come flying out of the darkness and claw at her hair. But there were no more bats, so she grabbed the raincoat and hat she'd discarded and headed back through the downpour to the trailer.

The lights were on in the front room. Through the window she could see Griffon pacing back and forth across the carpet, his hands clenched tightly at his sides, his shoulders hunched.

Rushing to the front door, she twisted the knob and barreled into the room, throwing her wet coat onto the floor as she ran. He looked up in surprise and then exclaimed something unintelligible as she hurled herself against him.

His arms came up to clasp her, and she pressed her face against his chest. "Matthew, I need you."

He pulled off her rain hat and combed his fingers through her hair. "I thought you wanted to be alone."

"I was afraid I was going to come apart. I'm back in control, sort of."

"I noticed that when we were still in our faxing phase, the way you won't give in to defeat."

"You're like that, too."

"No, I'm not."

"You're one of the top selling authors in the whole country! In the world, for that matter. You didn't get there by giving up. You got there because of your determination to survive—to more than survive."

He stared at her. "I never thought about it like that."

"Sometimes it takes an outside observer to put things in perspective. You keep doing that for me."

"Jessie, I'm not going to let you down."

At least until this is over, she thought as she turned and stared out the window into the darkness. With a little shiver, she broke away from him, crossed the room and pulled down the shade.

"You're right," he muttered. "Somebody could be watching us. One of them. Perry. Reva. Diedre. Edward."

"I realized this evening that Perry's got a motive." She recounted her new interpretation of the phone conversation she'd overheard.

"That sounds suggestive," Griffon agreed. "But he doesn't strike me as having the guts to murder someone."

"Which one of them does?"

He sighed. "You've got a point."

"Where's the bat?"

"In the freezer."

"To use an oft quoted phrase. Oh, yuck. Remind me not to eat any of your TV dinners—or drink your coffee."

"It's sealed up in a plastic carton."

She laughed. "I think you're going to have to throw the refrigerator away and start again."

"I'll take that under advisement."

A few minutes ago she'd been close to despair. But being with Matthew had helped. "Maybe we should both go back to the house and talk to them. Maybe somebody'll slip up and admit something.''

"Okay.'' He reached for the raincoat he'd left by the door.

They were halfway to the mansion when a pair of headlights cut through the darkness.

"Now what?'' Griffon muttered.

The car came to a bouncing stop in the parking area. Jessica gave a little start of surprise as a familiar figure scrambled out. It was Heather.

"What's wrong?'' Jessica shouted above the sound of the rain.

Heather pointed to the narrow lane. "I tried to drive back to the main road, but I couldn't get across the damn bridge.''

Jessica felt her throat tighten. "What do you mean? What's wrong with the bridge?''

"It's under a couple of feet of water. At least, that's what it looked like. I was going to try to cross anyway, but it's too deep.'' She gazed fearfully at the house and her voice rose to near hysteria. "So now we're trapped here. Nobody is going to get away. And the vampire is going to kill us all.''

Chapter Eleven

Matthew caught Jessica's startled expression—along with that of the young woman. "What vampire?" he snarled.

Heather's voice was barely above a whisper. "He warned me not to tell anyone."

"Who?"

"Him. You know. You…you brought him to life," she accused. "With your book."

Matthew advanced on the young woman, his eyes fierce. "What the hell are you talking about?"

Heather took a step back, looking as if she wished she could retract the bold statement.

"Dammit! You'd better explain," he shouted.

The young actress raised her chin. "You may think I'm an airhead, but I actually read *Midnight Kiss* before I got the script, to get some insights into the plot and characters. After I signed on for the movie, the vampire came to me. In my bedroom. Just like in your book."

"You're going to tell us about it." Jessica grabbed the young girl's hand and yanked her toward the dilapidated mansion looming in back of them.

Heather resisted, and Jessica bent, hissing something Matthew couldn't hear because the blood was roaring in his ears.

"You brought him to life." That's what she'd flung in his face. Then a dead man—with all the blood sucked out of his body—had shown up in Jessica's car. In some twisted way, had she assigned the blame to the right place?

Wanting more information, yet dreading what he was about to hear, he followed the two women into the house. Jessica's face was set in a rigid mask as she switched on the overhead light and gathered up a fistful of Heather's long hair, pulling her head back.

The illumination wasn't bright, but it exposed the gracefully arching column of the girl's neck. Strangely afraid of what he might find there, Matthew forced himself to look.

Both he and Jessica let out long, shuddering sighs. The milk-white skin was flawless. No puncture marks pierced the young woman's flesh the way he'd imagined.

"You're lying," Jessica practically snarled. "The vampire in the book didn't come to the girl's room to sit and drink diet soda with her. He came to sink his teeth into her neck and suck her blood. But not yours. Now suppose you tell us what's really going on."

"Okay. He didn't bite me," Heather whispered. "But he was going to. That's really why I wanted to leave this godforsaken house. And now we're all trapped."

An exclamation from the doorway made them all look up. Reva was there again.

"More spying?" Matthew tossed out, watching her face for some flicker of admission.

"No. I'm trying to protect myself," she said, projecting a note of terror it was hard to fault. He looked down to see a dagger in her hand. It glinted like polished silver, the metal that was supposed to kill vampires.

"Put that thing away before somebody gets hurt," he growled.

The secretary sucked in a sharp draft of air and let it out slowly as she slipped the knife into her belt.

"Protect yourself from what?" he demanded. "Don't tell us you've had some sort of nighttime visitor, too."

Her gaze skittered away from his. "It was last night after hearing about that homeless man. I thought it was a dream—because of what happened to him."

"All right, I want to know exactly what you experienced," Matthew declared. "Both of you. And everyone else in the cast who might be hiding some revelation because they think it's too crazy to share." He started toward the hall. "Are Edward and Diedre down here?"

"I think they're in their rooms," Reva replied.

"I'll get them," he told Jessica. "You take Heather and Reva to the den, and make sure Perry's still there. We're going to have a meeting."

She looked relieved to have him take charge, and he supposed he sounded as calm and in control as anyone could be under the circumstances. Maybe if he kept up the act, he would believe it himself. But he didn't think so. Not when he was fighting a nightmare vision that threatened to fill his mind like thick, choking smoke. Over and over he'd told Jessica there were no vampires. The mantra had been as much to convince himself as her. But what if somehow his twisted mind had brought the creatures of his imagination to life?

Jessica was still watching him, and his stomach knotted so tightly that he had to clench his fists to keep from grabbing his middle. Trying to show nothing on his face, he turned quickly and headed for the stairs.

As he went up, he concentrated on putting one foot in front of the other, willing his emotions to settle. He hadn't needed Heather's accusation to make him worry about what was really happening here.

As he climbed, he thought back to some of those long-ago sessions with Dr. Winters. The wise old doctor had gently pushed and prodded James Matthew Gregory into sharing his deepest fear—that his thoughts could affect reality. He'd been afraid of getting separated from his parents that day at the carnival. And he had—permanently. Dr. Winters had helped him understand that the things in your mind couldn't come to life. No matter how terrible they were, they only affected you. Nobody else.

Matthew stopped for a moment at the end of the hall, more or less back in control.

First he went to summon Diedre, since she might want a little time to get ready.

"Who is it?" she called out when he knocked on her door.

"Matthew Griffon. I'm sorry to disturb you, but we're having a meeting downstairs."

"At this hour? I've already retired," she said, using her most imperious stage voice.

"It's important."

"When I agreed to come out here, I didn't know I'd be required to be on duty so late in the evening."

"It's a safety meeting, and I'd appreciate your co-operation."

There was a long hesitation on the other side of the door during which he thought she might be dismissing him with her silence. Then he heard a rustle of clothing. A moment later, the barrier swung open. The actress was tying the belt of an elegant green silk dressing gown. The soft fabric clung to her well-preserved figure. But Matthew couldn't stop himself from staring at her face. When she'd gone to bed, she must have taken off the carefully applied makeup she'd been wearing earlier, and she looked as if she'd aged ten years since dinner.

"Everybody is assembling in the den," he said with stiff formality, wishing he hadn't had to invade her privacy.

"All right. I'll be down in a few minutes."

He turned away and headed for Vanesco's quarters at the other end of the hall. But although he rapped loudly, there was no answer.

"Edward?" he called out. "Are you all right?"

Still nothing. Good Lord, what else had happened while he'd kept Jessica in his bed this evening? Twisting the knob, he found that the door was locked.

Matthew rammed his shoulder against the barrier and felt the old lock give a little. He tried again, harder, and the antiquated mechanism gave with a groan. Inside, the lights were turned low, and it took a moment to get his bearing. Chair. Dresser. Closet. Bed. Edward was sprawled limply on top of the spread, fully clothed except for his shoes. His head lolled to one side, and one hand dangled toward the floor. Had the vampire gotten him, too?

Matthew made it to the bedside in three or four rapid strides. The first thing he noted was the smell of whiskey. Then he saw the empty bottle and overturned glass lying on the carpet.

"Edward."

The only answer from the former matinee idol was a deep snore. He lay with his mouth open, his jaw slack and his eyes closed.

"Wake up." Roughly, Matthew shook the limp body, but the effect was negligible. "Damn."

Well, now he knew why the two senior members of the cast had disappeared so early. Diedre couldn't face the strain of an evening with the rest of the merry band. Neither could Edward. In fact, he couldn't even face an evening with himself.

Matthew kicked the empty bottle into the corner, venting some of the frustration that had been building inside him. Then, with a sigh, he turned and headed back downstairs.

Ten minutes later, everyone except Vanesco was dutifully present and accounted for in the den. With an absolutely straight face, Matthew explained that he'd found the actor soundly asleep and hadn't wanted to wake him.

"Drunk, probably." Perry tossed the words into the

quizzical silence. "There have been rumors about the old guy for years."

"Maybe so. But he's also been under a lot of pressure," Diedre put in.

"You look like you have, too," the younger man shot back.

Her papery skin lost even more of its color.

"All right." Jessica's voice cut through the thickening atmosphere in the room like a scalpel. "We're not here to insult each other. We're here to exchange information."

"What if some of us aren't interested in participating?" Perry asked.

"I suggest you get interested," Matthew interjected. "Because, for starters, whether you like it or not, we're going to have to get along with each other for the next few days. The river's flooded. Apparently it's over the bridge."

Perry stood, his challenging gaze fixed on Matthew. "I'm going to call the authorities. There must be some other way to get us out of here. By helicopter, or boat, for example."

Before anyone could object, he stalked out of the room. However, he was back before they'd had a chance to resume the meeting. "The phone is dead."

JESSICA WATCHED the room empty, as the cast members dispersed to check the various other extensions in the house. She turned to Matthew, catching hold of his arm. He slipped his arm around her waist. They stood silently and still until the others had disappeared down the hall.

"I don't like this," she whispered.

"The river's damn bad luck. The phones..." His voice trailed off. Apparently he wasn't up to false reassurances.

"They were okay this afternoon. I know, because I called Dan to see if there were any further developments in the murder case."

"Were there?"

"No."

"What time was it?" he asked.

"Before you came in to dinner."

"Did you get any calls after that?"

"No. But I only gave the number to Dan."

"Right."

"What if someone's cut the lines?" Jessica's voice quavered.

"We've still got the cellular units."

"Not mine. I've got a rental car." She tried to imitate the strong, steady tone of his voice. "Would you check the one in the camper?"

Griffon squeezed her hand reassuringly. "Sure."

The feeling of reassurance vanished when he disappeared into the rain, and a prickling sensation clawed at the back of Jessica's neck as she imagined a supernatural figure materializing out of the darkness. Then she changed the image to a shoddy trick shot in a cheap horror flick. They weren't being stalked by a vampire. Some living, breathing person was stalking them. And she could prove it. Instead of standing and waiting for Griffon at the back door, she turned and rushed up the stairs to her room. Slamming the door she rummaged in her suitcase. For a moment she thought the thing she sought had been stolen, and she cursed softly under her breath. But she kept on looking. Finally her fingers encountered silky fabric tucked into one of the compartments. Slipping it into her pocket, she returned to the kitchen.

Griffon was back quickly, his face grim. "My phone's inoperable," he reported. "I can't figure out why it's not working. It's a new model I had installed before leaving Maine."

"How long has it been out of order?" Jessica asked, unconsciously lowering her voice as if the walls had ears.

"I haven't used it since yesterday."

"Was the camper locked?"

"Of course. Except when I was inside."

The clipped conversation was interrupted as Perry poked his head into the kitchen. "What the hell are you whispering about behind our backs?" he growled, his voice giving away the panic he'd managed to keep off his face.

"Sorry," Jessica apologized. "Matthew's just come back from checking the telephone in his camper."

"And?"

"It's out of order, too."

"How inconvenient." He wheeled and disappeared down the hall.

Jessica and Matthew followed him into the den where they all took seats. Jessica peered around at the circle of faces. Perry looked hostile, the women anxious.

"The phone in the camper is out of order," Matthew told the group. "What about the ones in here?"

"What do you think?" Reva challenged.

"I'm not clairvoyant."

"Well, the line to the house is dead," she retorted.

"Maybe it was shorted by all the rain," Diedre suggested.

"Or *he* may have done it," Heather hedged. "Because now he has us at his mercy."

"He?" the older actress asked.

"The vampire," Heather clarified.

Perry cursed.

Diedre gasped.

Reva looked almost triumphant.

Jessica's gaze slid to Griffon. He was leaning back comfortably in one of the armchairs. But she could see the tension etched around his eyes and mouth. She wanted to go to him, cling to him, as much for her own comfort as his. Instead she faced the group.

"Let's not get all wound up with the supernatural."

"Do you have a better suggestion?" Perry asked.

"Bear with me for a minute," she said. "How many of you have read *Midnight Kiss*?"

Surprisingly, everyone in the room raised a hand. Well, at least they were conscientious. Or perhaps they'd each been looking for insights into their characters—an edge that would make their part the most memorable in the film.

"We all know the book is about a vampire who comes to women in the night, playing on their longings for intimacy in order to—to feed." She paused and looked at Griffon. He was sitting as still as a statue. "Heather and Reva have reported nighttime visitations similar to those described in the book. And it happened to me, too. Has anyone else had a comparable experience?''

For a moment there was shocked silence. Then Diedre's fingers flickered, and her hand went halfway up.

Jessica glanced from her to the other women. They were all looking at each other apprehensively and with newly appraising eyes.

"Well, my visit wasn't from a real vampire," Jessica said. "It was someone pretending to be one."

"How do you know?" Perry challenged.

"Let me set the scene first. I'd come out to inspect the mansion—to see if it was suitable for the movie." Jessica glanced at Griffon again. He looked wary, as if he were wondering just how far she was going to go. She tried to send him a reassuring look. "I'd arranged to meet Richie out here, but I didn't know Griffon would be coming, too. After Richie, uh, left, Griffon and I were caught in a storm and ended up in his camper. It was raining too hard to get back to my car, so I spent the night there," she went on quickly, aware that everyone was watching the two of them with new interest.

"Griffon lent me his bedroom and slept in the living room."

Perry snorted. "Oh, yeah, like tonight when you went out there?"

She shot him an angry look but she didn't dignify his comment with an explanation.

Griffon's features were frozen into an unreadable mask.

"I woke up in the morning to see wings fluttering against the window. And a soft, seductive voice calling me to destruction,'' Jessica continued. ''It was like a thread was pulling me forward, reeling me in.''

''Yes!'' Heather breathed.

''Can any of the rest of you add something to that general description?'' Jessica asked.

''I was going to open the window. Then I came back to my senses,'' Diedre murmured.

Jessica's frank admission had broken the ice. All at once, the other women wanted to share an experience that they'd instinctively kept hidden.

''It was like being seduced by a lover,'' Diedre said. ''He made me feel young and desirable.''

''I kept looking at my neck to make sure he hadn't bitten me,'' Heather whispered.

Jessica gave each member of the group time to speak her piece. ''None of the men were visited?'' she clarified.

Griffon shook his head.

''Not me,'' Perry snapped. ''And if it had happened to Edward, he probably wouldn't remember.''

Jessica asked the women for dates and times. The visits had all occurred in the past week and a half.

''He's come after all of us,'' Heather whispered. ''Since we signed on for the movie.''

''Someone's been playing with our minds,'' Jessica agreed. ''But not a vampire. When Griffon and I talked about it, we figured out that whoever it was had been using standard hypnotic induction techniques on me.''

''Can you prove it?'' Perry asked.

''How can you prove something like that? But there's more concrete evidence it wasn't a supernatural visitation. After it happened to me, Matthew and I went out to have a look. The storm had washed the ground clean, but there were tracks leading toward the trailer and then back into the woods.''

"Footprints?" Diedre asked hopefully.

"Nothing so prosaic. They were prints that looked like a goat walking on two legs. Tracks designed to fool us into thinking it wasn't a person. But it was, of course. No matter what the perpetrator wanted us to think."

"How do you know it was a person?" Diedre challenged.

"Because whoever was at the camper that morning dropped this," Jessica said as she whipped the black scarf out of her pocket and waved it in the air for everyone to see.

Heather snatched the rectangle away and ran the silky fabric through her fingers. "I wish this proved something," she said.

"It does."

"No. It only proves that someone or something was there. Suppose it *was* a vampire. He couldn't go around naked. He'd wear clothes just like everyone else. And he could have brought the scarf to wrap around your neck when he was finished. To hide the bites."

Chapter Twelve

Jessica stared at her, feeling reality shift and twist. She and Griffon had both been so sure what the black silk meant. But Heather had deftly supplied a different interpretation.

"Well, this is just great." Perry muttered. "I suppose the next thing we're going to find out is that the bat that attacked Jessica on the porch was a vampire bat."

"It *was* a vampire bat!" Heather said.

Jessica turned to stare at her. "Stop putting the worst possible slant on everything that happens."

The young woman flushed. "I—I'm sorry. I didn't want to say anything before. But I knew what it was as soon as I saw it. That's when I decided to get out of here."

"You're asking us to believe you're an expert on bats?" Perry snorted.

She glared at him. "We studied them in school last year. Vampire bats are very distinctive looking. They live in South and Central America, and they're bigger than the ones around here. They have that U-shaped pad at the end of their muzzle and those long legs so they can climb up on animals and suck their blood. Gross!"

"You only got a glimpse of it," Jessica objected. "You could be wrong." She slid her gaze to Griffon, hoping he'd back her up.

"She's right," he said quietly. "I thought it might be, so I went back to the trailer and looked it up in a book."

"Why didn't you tell me?" Jessica demanded.

"I didn't see any point in supplying something else to worry about."

"If it's from South America, how did it get on the porch?" Diedre wondered aloud.

"Someone deliberately brought it here, knowing it was going to frighten one of us. Or maybe they specifically went after me," Jessica answered as she peered at the circle of faces around her. They all registered varying degrees of shock, disgust and skepticism. But then, they were a group of actors, she reminded herself.

"So let me clarify the situation," Reva said. "We're trapped in this house for nobody knows how long, with either a vampire or a nut."

"It's not a vampire." Griffon's hard-edged voice rose above the general babble that had sprung up. "Notice Jessica was visited at my trailer, not her highrise apartment. So the perpetrator only had to walk up to the window."

"At my house, too," Diedre said. "I live in a ranch."

Griffon turned to Heather. "And you?"

"My bedroom used to be the recreation room of

our house. It's in the basement, with a sliding glass door to the outside.''

"Another easy approach," Griffon said.

"But what about me?" Reva argued. "I'm in a high rise. On the fourth floor."

"Do you have a balcony?" Griffon asked. "Is it close to your neighbors?"

Reva reluctantly nodded.

"That's one way to do it. Or if someone had a key, they could have gotten inside. Was your door bolted?"

"It was after I was visited," she snapped. "And I'd still like to hear your explanation of the footprints you saw. You said they looked like goat feet. Didn't the monsters in *The Haunting of Greg Matthews* have cloven hooves?"

Griffon looked startled. "You read it?"

"I started with *Midnight Kiss*. When I finished with that one, I wanted to know what Jessica was really getting into, so I perused all your stuff. You've got one sick imagination. It's like you're courting the forces of evil, inviting them into your life. If anyone was going to attract vampires or werewolves or devils with strange footprints, it would be you, buddy."

Jessica saw Griffon's face go pale. "That's a ridiculous accusation," she told her secretary. "We've got enough problems without hearing nonsense like that." Yet even as she spoke, she saw the rest of the group was eyeing Griffon with new suspicion.

"Does anyone have a gun?" Perry asked.

"Don't be an ass. Guns won't do you any good against vampires," Heather mocked him. "Unless you brought along a supply of silver bullets."

"Well, there's always garlic," Diedre said.

Jessica regarded the tense faces, knowing she was seeing these people fall apart under pressure. "I'm beginning to get a good idea of how mass hysteria starts," she commented. "Or maybe mass paranoia. I think we're all so strung out and exhausted that we're getting on each other's nerves. Why don't we get a good night's sleep and meet again in the morning? For all we know, the river could be down by then, and we can leave."

"Permanently," Perry growled. "If you think I'm going to keep working on this project, you're insane."

He'd pushed one of her buttons. "That's what you wanted all along, isn't it? Are you the one terrifying the cast and crew so you can close the production down?" The moment the words were out of her mouth, she wished she could call them back.

Perry glared at her. Everyone else waited for an explanation.

"I'm sorry. I know you want out of your contract. And I guess I'm just as anxious as everyone else to find a scapegoat," she mumbled.

"We're all on edge," Diedre agreed. "You're right. We should call it a night."

"I'm not sleeping alone in this house," Heather wailed. "It's not safe."

Perry gave her a sardonic look. "You've been trying to get me into bed with you since this production began. Now you've finally got an excuse."

"Stop it!" Jessica flared. "Don't you realize that cutting each other down isn't going to help? We can move some furniture around and sleep dormitory style. The men together and the women.''

"Oh, no, we can't. I want Mr. Griffon out of the house tonight and back in his trailer,'' Reva said. "And the door locked behind him.''

Jessica could hardly believe what she'd heard. "What?''

"I'm not going to sleep a wink if I know he's under the same roof with me,'' she insisted.

Matthew stood, his features grim as he started for the door. "That suits me just fine.''

Jessica crossed to him and grabbed his arm. "Don't leave yet.'' Her fingers dug into his flesh. When she realized how tightly she was holding him, she eased up a little.

He gave her a long look, waiting.

"Perry, you can sleep in Edward's room if you want,'' she said. "Or in your own. But I'd like you to help us move some beds around for the others. I think Diedre's room is the biggest. She and Reva and Heather can sleep there. Is that satisfactory?''

They agreed with varying levels of enthusiasm.

"Where does that leave you?'' Reva asked Jessica.

"If Matthew's going to the camper, so am I. He and I have to talk.''

Perry leered at them "I've been around the block a few times, and I know damn well when a man and a woman are doing a lot more than talking. Did his sexy vampire turn you on? Was that why you wanted him down here for the filming?''

Heat flooded Jessica's face, but she knew any answer she gave would make things worse.

Hands balled into fists, Griffon started toward the young actor. "I'm tired of your smutty comments. You're quite the man of experience, aren't you? Are you speaking as the pot head who was busted for possession? Or the gambling freak who needs money to pay off his Atlantic City debts?" he asked icily.

Perry blanched but recovered enough to retort, "What did you do, have me checked out? And everybody else, too?" He turned to the group. "How do you like that folks? Mr. Griffon thinks he's Sherlock Holmes."

"I like to know what kind of scum I'm dealing with," Griffon shot back.

"Is that what you think of us?" Diedre asked.

Griffon turned to her. "I'm sorry. That didn't come out quite right. I wasn't talking about you."

"Now I *really* don't want you in the house," Reva muttered.

"You never did. Probably because—" This time he caught himself and stopped.

"Because what?" Reva challenged.

"Forget it. I'm letting my mouth get ahead of my brain."

Jessica's assistant stood with her hands on her hips. "I'd like to hear what you have to say."

"I think we've had enough for tonight," Jessica interjected. "We all passed the point of self-control a long time ago. Let's go to sleep."

Reva gave her a mocking smile. "Oh, I'm sure it's going to be quite a restful night."

After making sure that everyone got settled, Jessica went to her own room to grab a toothbrush. Then she shrugged and stuffed everything she'd unpacked back into her suitcase. For all she knew, she'd find herself still locked out of the house in the morning.

As she stepped out of her room, she saw Griffon coming down the hall, his shoulders slumped. When he saw her, he straightened.

Her emotions were in so much turmoil that she blurted the question that had been deviling her. "Why didn't you tell me that the cloven hooves were in *Greg Matthews?*" she asked.

"You read the book!"

"I skimmed some parts." She was having trouble keeping her voice from rising.

"And used the material to drag information out of me."

She could feel the muscles of her face freezing into place as they stood looking at each other. Griffon's expression was similar. From somewhere down the hallway, she heard a door open. Then Reva was gliding toward them looking entirely too pleased to hear them at odds.

"If you're leaving, you'd better do it so I can lock up," she said to Jessica.

"Maybe you should stay here," Griffon said.

"No."

She wasn't sure what he would have said if Reva hadn't been watching them with such avid interest. As if the matter were settled, she took his arm. When she hefted her suitcase awkwardly in her other hand, he reached over and took it from her.

The three of them descended the steps.

"Good luck," Jessica said to her assistant as they reached the back door.

Reva nodded. "You, too." She cleared her throat. "I'm sorry I flew off the handle at the meeting. It was the tension, you know."

"We're all under a lot of strain," Jessica replied.

Reva looked abashed. "I don't…uh…have to lock the door."

"Go ahead and do it," Griffon insisted. "It's safer."

"What time do you want to come back?"

Jessica considered the question. "Maybe the best thing for everyone's nerves is to try to maintain a normal schedule. What if we come over for breakfast at eight-thirty? Then we can get to work at nine-thirty."

"That sounds okay—if you can get everyone to cooperate."

"If you and Griffon back me up."

"You can count on me."

Reva looked so contrite that Jessica held out her arms. The redhead came into them, and they embraced.

"I'm sorry all this is happening to you," Reva whispered. "And that I'm not helping," she added after a little pause.

Jessica gave her a tighter squeeze. "It'll be all right."

Griffon didn't speak again until they were well away from the house. "Reva should get an Oscar for that performance."

"Why?"

"She wants to make you think she's on your side."

"You don't believe that?"

"I've caught the looks she gives you when she thinks nobody's watching."

"What kind of looks?"

"Malicious." Griffon clarified. "She hates you."

"I don't believe that. She's just under a lot of tension."

"Instead of making excuses for one of our happy little crew, you'd better be suspicious of everyone."

"Even you?"

"Especially me. I'm the dark prince who brings the forces of evil into this world."

She stopped and faced him. "Is that what's been eating at you? Heather's and Reva's half-baked comments?"

"*You* asked the question."

"I'm exhausted. And worried. Cut me some slack."

He unlocked the door and stepped aside so she could enter the trailer.

After tossing her bag onto the rug, Jessica flopped onto the couch. "God, what a zoo. Every time I thought we'd settled an issue, someone would pop up with another frightening possibility. What do you think about Reva being in a high rise?"

"You've already heard what I think about Reva. You just don't want to listen."

Jessica was so wound up she couldn't stop talking. "You know, I kept feeling like I'd heard this before. Now I remember where. Did you see *The Invasion of the Body Snatchers?* Not the one with Donald Sutherland. The first version with a group of people trapped in a small town. Starring Dana Winters and

Kevin McCarthy. Remember, they gave him a cameo in the remake? Anyway, the people know that if they go to sleep, the aliens will take over their bodies. So they have to stay awake. And they get more and more irrational. Maybe if we live through this, we can use it for a movie plot." She stopped babbling and laughed hollowly. "Perry was the worst, I guess. But I'm not sure how to deal with Heather."

"We're not in any shape to make decisions tonight. We both need some rest. You can have the bedroom, I'll take the couch," he said wearily.

She stared up at him. "I don't think anyone's coming out here to check on us. Besides, they're probably as astute as Perry, anyway."

His face was etched in granite. "What I think is that our relationship has been getting too intense too fast."

His words were like a blow to the solar plexus. She gasped and folded in the middle. Yet, even as she sat there clutching her fists to her abdomen, she knew what was really happening.

"Stop it," she managed to say.

He turned away.

She pictured herself going to him, slipping her arms around his waist the way she'd done before, making him realize he didn't have to protect her by pushing her away.

But in her present exhausted state, she simply couldn't cope with another one of his rebuffs. She was the one who'd been breathing life into this relationship. Maybe she'd been making a stupid mistake all along.

Slowly she got up to retrieve her luggage.

"Matthew?" She wasn't sure whether she'd spoken aloud or whether her mind whispered his name. She only knew he didn't turn around and that the room felt suddenly ten degrees colder.

As she hoisted the strap of her bag over her shoulder, the world seemed to sway around her, and she had to reach out and steady herself against the wall. When the moment of dizziness passed, she started down the hall to the bedroom where they'd made love only hours before.

Her vision blurred. By the time she closed the door, kicked off her shoes and threw herself onto the bed, tears were streaming down her cheeks. She wanted to run down the hall and scream at him. She wanted to tell him that part of his problem was that he'd married the wrong woman—that he wouldn't have been arguing with Gwen if she'd been proud of his talent as a writer of popular fiction and not tried to push him into an academic career that was all wrong for him. But what good would any of that do? He'd only see it as an attack on his dead wife.

Instead she rolled onto her back and lay weeping quietly in the darkness.

SHE MUST HAVE dozed off, because there was no transition from her feeling of impotent misery to the sound of waves gently breaking against a familiar shore. It was like the tape from her childhood. Like the night the vampire had visited.

Matthew had told her she was supposed to do something if she heard the waves, but she couldn't remember what. Instead she smiled, letting the ebb and flow rock her as she snuggled deeper under the covers.

Soon the soothing sound was overlaid by a seductive whisper. At first she couldn't make out the words, only a low buzz that brought her a feeling of great peace. Then the buzz resolved itself into a voice coming from somewhere above her head.

"Jessica, Jessica, it's time. Let me into your mind, sweet."

She knew instantly who was calling her. "No," she murmured thickly.

"Don't fight me, Jessica. It will be much easier for you if you just let yourself go. Like falling off the side of your father's swimming pool and into the cool, clear water."

"My father?" She tried to open her eyes. Somehow, she couldn't make the lids work properly. Lying motionless in bed, she strained her ears and caught the sound of wings fluttering in the air. Not outside the window. There was another presence in the darkened room with her. Something wicked.

Her hands clenched and unclenched. She was supposed to dig her nails—

"Jessica, I'm here."

The wispy thought about her nails merged into the mist that wrapped her mind.

"Go away. Leave me alone, for God's sake," she whispered, yet she couldn't put any force behind her words.

The vampire laughed, high and shrill. "You got away from me the last time you slept alone in Matthew

Griffon's bed. But this time is different. This time you don't have what it takes to fight me, do you?''

She tried to push herself up, to wake. But it was no good; she could sense her feeble resistance crumbling.

The laugh came again, more sardonic, more assured. ''Griffon wants to end the relationship. You've only made a fool of yourself letting him enjoy your body.''

Jessica squeezed her eyes shut, as if that could block out the voice buzzing like a saw, cutting through the cells of her brain.

''Griffon is self-centered and arrogant. He's evil. He's the cause of all your problems. If you hadn't decided to film his cursed book, you wouldn't be trapped here with a bunch of sniveling fools.''

You're lying, her mind screamed as she tried to cringe away from the hateful words.

Her breath was coming in jagged little pants as she writhed and twisted on the tangled bedclothes, her hands clenching and unclenching.

''Matthew Griffon played with your head. Matthew Griffon used you. Matthew Griffon is evil,'' the vampire continued. ''Think of all the heartache and terror he's unleashed on mankind with his wicked books. I wouldn't be here now, talking to you if he hadn't invented me.''

The vampire seemed to draw closer. ''But you can stop him. You can keep him from hurting anyone else. He's right down the hall—in the living room. Go out there and put an end to his miserable life,'' the voice in her head commanded.

Jessica's whole body jerked as she recoiled from the

order. "No!" she screamed. At least it sounded like a scream as it echoed inside her head.

"Killing him is so easy. He's made it easy. Almost as if that's what he wants you to do, because he knows how wicked he is. There's a gun in the bottom left-hand drawer of his desk. It's loaded. All you have to do is aim and fire."

Jessica shook her head violently and dug her fingers into the tangled bedclothes. But her body was out of her control. Horrified, as if she were in the corner of the room watching some other woman, she saw herself get off the bed and stand for a moment swaying in the darkness.

"Good. Good. Now cross the room and start down the hall." To Matthew. Yes, she wanted to go to him.

On legs that felt like blocks of wood she moved down the hall toward the front of the camper. Toward Matthew.

There was a dim light shining over the kitchen sink, and her throat worked convulsively when she saw him lying on the sofa, his knees drawn up against his chest.

"Matthew. Oh God, Matthew, wake up. Don't let me do this to you." She felt herself calling him, but she heard no sound except the padding of her bare feet as she crossed the carpet. When she reached the desk, she knelt.

"In the bottom drawer. Get the gun." The voice was low but commanding. "Use it on him!"

Jessica was still fighting, still struggling for control. With trembling fingers she reached into the drawer and brought out a revolver. It felt heavy and foreign in her hand. She didn't want to be holding it. Still, with a little moan, she turned and pointed the weapon at Matthew.

Chapter Thirteen

The hand that held the gun shook.

"That's right, sweet," the relentless voice said. "Now squeeze the trigger. You know he's a bastard. He's lied to you, and hurt you. When he's dead, all your troubles will be over. And his, too."

Even as Jessica struggled to bring her actions under her own control, she felt the muscles of her free hand contract, felt her nails dig painfully into her flesh. The sudden sting sent a shudder through her body—and a jolt to her brain.

"No! No, I won't. Matthew, wake up. Get out of the way." This time she heard her agonized protest echo in the room.

"Do it! Damn you, do it."

As the vampire's shrill voice cried out the order, Griffon moved like a wild animal suddenly released from a cage, rolling off the couch and onto the floor, out of Jessica's line of sight.

"Do it! What's wrong with you, you bitch? Do it?" The voice and tone of the command had changed from smooth and persuasive to shrill and angry.

Utterly confused, Jessica stood in the middle of the

carpet. But her mind was focused on one task now. A shuddering sigh rattled in her chest as she forced the hand with the gun to open. The weapon dangled and swayed dangerously in her grasp.

As if by magic, Griffon was beside her, lifting the weapon out of her hand before she dropped it on the floor where it could go off by accident.

She remained unmoving, disoriented, in the center of the room. If Matthew didn't tell her what to do, she might stand there forever. ''The vam-vampire...'' she stammered weakly.

He cradled his arm around her shoulder. His touch released her, and she began to shake all over, her teeth chattering uncontrollably.

''Come on,'' Griffon urged as he steered her toward the sofa. The world was still disjointed, so that she had no memory of crossing the room. The next thing she knew, she was sitting down and he was beside her. She turned toward him, wedging her hand against his chest, feeling the steady beat of his heart. She didn't think she'd fired the gun, but she needed to know that he was safe and unharmed—that she hadn't done the unthinkable when the gun was in her hand. ''Are you all right?''

''Are you?''

''Yes,'' she lied.

She laid her head against his shoulder, as her hands stroked over his strong arms and across the broad expanse of his back.

The vampire's words came back, and her nails dug into his biceps. ''Oh, Matthew, it knew we had a fight. It used that.''

A curse rumbled in his chest.

"It...told me where to find the gun. I took it out of the drawer. I almost shot you."

"But you didn't," he soothed, chafing one of her icy hands in his. "Instead you shouted a warning."

"Yes." She marveled at that. In the last terrible moment, she'd broken free of the vampire's spell. That was something, anyway. She gripped his arms. "I have to tell you—we have to—"

Before she could finish, he pressed his fingers over her mouth. "No," he whispered close to her ear. "Someone might hear."

Jessica looked around in alarm, her eyes going to the door and then to the window.

"This place is bugged," he said in a low voice as he got to his feet. When he started for the bedroom, she followed.

Standing on the bed and crushing down the pillows with his bare feet, he began to run his hand behind the light fixture near the ceiling. "That wasn't some supernatural bogeyman giving you directions from another astral plane," he told her. "I heard it, too."

As she grappled with that, he went on, his tone very low. "I woke up when you came down the hall, Jessie. I heard a voice telling you what a bastard I was, and that if you killed me, all your troubles would be over."

"Why didn't you move?" she gasped.

He didn't answer. Then he turned to the light and resumed the search.

She stood watching him, bursting with the need to communicate, yet holding back the words out of necessity. Gritting her teeth, she forced herself to think.

She'd been asleep, and the vampire had wakened her. Griffon said it was coming from a speaker. Did that mean the device was near the head of the bed?

That was logical, but the voice had been just as strong as she'd walked down the hall.

When she got up and started toward the door, Griffon gave her a questioning look. "Be right back."

In the hall, she dropped to her knees and began to feel along the edge of the carpet, trying first one side and then the other. Disappointed when she didn't find anything, she stood and gazed along the line where the ceiling met the wall. About halfway toward the living room was a light fixture. First she felt around the bulb. Then she swept her fingers over the top. At the back was a rounded lump that didn't seem to belong on the curved metal surface. Her heart started to pound as she pulled the object free and held it in the palm of her hand, turning it this way and that. It looked a little like part of a water faucet.

When she reached the bedroom and held up the device to Griffon, he was beside her in an instant, lifting it from her hand and holding it up to the light.

"Where?" he mouthed.

"Hall light."

Muttering an imprecation, he dropped it to the floor and ground it under his foot. Then he turned and surveyed the bedroom again, looking at the places he'd searched and those he'd missed.

Jessica saw him stop and focus on the light in the center of the ceiling. It wasn't easily accessible from the end of the bed—or anywhere else. Pulling over the chair from the corner, he climbed up, unscrewed the cover from the fixture and began to feel around the rim. In seconds he was holding a twin to the device Jessica had discovered in the hall. It suffered the same fate as the other one.

But they still couldn't discuss anything important. If they'd found two of these things, there could be more in the camper.

In exasperation, Jessica flattened the palm of her hand and did an imitation of writing on it with her index finger.

Griffon nodded and pulled a pad of paper and a ballpoint pen from the bedside table.

"Have to talk." She penned the words, then stopped to consider their options. "Carriage house?"

Griffon nodded.

Jessica tapped his arm. When he looked at her questioningly, she wrote "False impression."

He nodded his understanding, and she began to speak, her voice pitched to sound as though she were too weary to cope with the unfolding circumstances— and as if she were blaming Matthew. "I don't know about you, but I'm not in any shape to try to deal with this tonight. All I want to do is get some sleep. I know you're afraid to have anyone hear us, but nobody can listen to us if we're not talking."

"You always get the last word," he agreed, his own tone sardonic.

"Well, this time it's good-night!"

"That suits me just fine."

The angry words flying back and forth between them made her light-headed. This was too much like the way they'd been a few hours before. Jessica's vision blurred, and she raised her eyes to Griffon's, hoping he could see how much this hurt.

His expression was fierce, and her name was like a strangled whisper on his lips. He took a step forward. So did she. Then he enfolded her with his strong arms and the blessed warmth of his body. She clung to him tightly, tipping her face up, her lips questing for his. When they met, she felt an inarticulate cry from deep inside him.

"Matthew. Matthew," she murmured as her lips moved against his, seeking reassurances even as she tried to tell him wordlessly that she loved him—that none of her feelings had changed.

The kiss went on and on, each of them devouring the other's mouth. Each of them moving and shifting, touching and holding, reassuring and exciting. There was so much they needed to say. Yet the only way they could communicate now was through the purely physical.

His hands stroked the length of her body, greedily tracing the curve of her waist, shaping the roundness of her hips. When he finally lifted his mouth, they were both breathing hard. She locked her arms around him, and buried her face in his shirt, vividly aware of her own arousal—and his. It was like a thick, heavy cloak, enfolding them, sheltering them from hurt and danger. All she had to do was push him just a little further, and he would carry her the few feet to the waiting bed. For a little while he would wipe everything from her mind but the joy of making love with him. Yet she knew they didn't have that luxury. Not if they were going to outwit whoever was trying to destroy them.

When she looked up and saw the frustration and regret in his eyes, she felt her chest tighten.

"We'd better go," he whispered.

She nodded but held him close for a few precious moments longer, storing up sensations. Then she commanded herself to pull away.

Griffon squeezed her shoulder before beginning to move quietly around the camper, gathering supplies— including a rolled sleeping bag. The rest he stuffed into a blue knapsack. She followed him into the living room, and he gave her a meaningful look as he picked up the gun.

Jessica wished they didn't need it, but it gave her a feeling of security as he slipped it into the pocket of the knapsack.

They stepped outside into the chilly morning mist. Miraculously the rain had stopped, but it was still damp—the humidity like cotton batting pressing against her lungs. Or maybe the breathless sensation came from fear. Leaving the camper had seemed like a good idea a few minutes ago. In fact, it had been her suggestion. Now the night felt alive with menace—the air thick with danger.

Jessica strained to see through the darkness, feeling exposed and vulnerable—as if someone might be watching her through infrared glasses or a rifle sight. She slid her gaze to Griffon. After pausing to lock the door, he circled her shoulder with his arm. Gratefully she moved closer to the shelter of his body as she looked across at the mansion. Everyone else on the

estate was supposed to be locked up safe and sound—
at Reva's instigation. Yet Jessica couldn't stop her
from probing the shadows that swathed the Victorian
building. Was someone lurking in the shrubbery,
watching them leave the camper?

Forcing that thought from her mind, she shifted her
inspection to the upstairs windows of the house. They
were all dark. So the others were still asleep. Or lying
in bed wondering what was going to happen next. Or
dead.

Perhaps Griffon heard the catch in her breath.
"Let's go," he urged.

Together they made their way slowly toward the
woods, each of them stumbling more than once on the
uneven ground.

When they stepped under the overhanging branches,
the darkness seemed to swallow them up. Then Griffon switched on the flashlight.

"Thanks," Jessica murmured.

He kept the beam angled low. "The foliage should
hide the light."

Neither of them spoke again as they picked their
way over tree roots and around giant puddles. The
sound of their shoes squishing on the pine needles was
accompanied only by water dripping from the trees.

The farther they got from the camper, the harder it
was for Jessica to hold back what she needed to
say. "I'm sorry," she finally blurted as they came out
from under the trees.

"About pointing the gun at me?"

"Yes," she whispered.

"It wasn't your fault. That voice put you into another hypnotic trance."

"I thought you couldn't do something under hypnosis that you wouldn't ordinarily do."

"Maybe you really did want to kill me." He laughed harshly in the darkness.

"Don't joke about it. It was awful. I didn't want to pick up the gun. I kept trying to stop, but I couldn't get control."

"But you did—when it counted. The important thing is that you didn't shoot."

Jessica sucked in a shaky breath and let it out slowly. She supposed he was right. She had wanted to go to Matthew, and so in that sense she hadn't been acting against her desires. And she hadn't shot him. Thank the Lord.

"You're cold. We'd better get inside." He tugged her forward.

As she moved with him, she suddenly realized there was a sound she'd been hearing in the background since they'd stepped outside the camper. Stopping, she cocked her head and listened more intently. It was running water. Swift running water—wild and menacing, almost like a living thing crashing through the woods looking for prey.

"Do you hear the river?" she asked.

"Yeah. The current must be pretty strong after all that rain."

"I wonder how high it is. Do you think the carriage house is safe?"

He shrugged. "We'll find out."

Finally they stepped out of the trees onto a cracked

driveway. A gray dawn was breaking, and Jessica breathed a sigh of relief as she spotted the old building.

Griffon detached his arm from around her shoulder. ''Wait here.''

Jessica watched him yank on the door. It creaked open on rusty hinges, and she stood tensely as he disappeared inside. He'd told her to stay where she was, instead she tiptoed toward the yawning opening, listening intently, but all she could hear was the raging water.

Seconds ticked by, and she felt her chest tighten painfully. ''Matthew!''

He was outside before she could blink. ''Are you all right?''

''I needed to know you were.''

''Everything's fine, come on in.''

It wasn't really any warmer in the old building than in the woods, but at least it was dryer. Jessica watched as Griffon played the light around the dusty, disused interior.

''Nobody's been here in years, as far as I can see.'' The beam fell on several ancient cars, a wagon and a sleigh. All were grimy and covered with spiderwebs.

Griffon's pack and the sleeping bag sat in the center of the brick floor. Turning, he spread out the latter. ''We can sit on this.''

''Yes. Thanks.''

She snuggled close to him, thankful for the protective weight of his arm around her shoulder. She had told *him* she was sorry, and she wished he'd tell *her* how he really felt about what had happened. But his next question was strictly business.

"The voice you heard talking to me, was it a woman?" she asked.

"It was disguised and I couldn't hear it that well."

"Actors are trained to use different voices. What about Perry? He was certainly nasty enough last night."

Griffon flipped the sleeping bag's zipper tab. "He's my second choice. But I like Reva better."

"You've been prejudiced against her from the beginning."

"I wouldn't call it prejudice. More like justifiable suspicion. She was at the door listening after the rehearsal session. She was also at the door after the bat incident. She lives in a building where it would be very hard for a make-believe vampire to get at her, yet she claims she was visited just like the other women. So I say she's lying. And one more thing. She volunteered to get the house ready before everyone else arrived. She was out here alone for a whole day. And I left the camper here part of the time."

Jessica considered the evidence. "I can understand your logic, but why would she be doing all of that? I mean, what's her motive?"

He shrugged. "That's what I can't figure out. So I think the next thing to do is search her luggage. At eight-thirty, we'll go back to the house. You'll keep everybody busy, and I'll slip upstairs."

"And how do I do that?"

His voice turned hard. "By telling the enthralling story of what happened this morning. The vampire whispers, the gun, the bugs. The whole bit. That should—''

He was cut off by a scream of terror that sliced through the air outside the carriage house like a sharp knife though living flesh.

Chapter Fourteen

Griffon leapt up and made for the door. Jessica took off right behind him. For agonizing seconds, she saw nothing. Then a running figure appeared.

It was Reva, tearing through the underbrush, her bright scarlet robe streaming out behind her like tongues of flame.

"The vampire. The vampire," she screamed in terror as she drew near the carriage house.

"Wait," Jessica called, dashing toward her. "It's not a vampire. We heard it, too. There were microphones in the trailer."

But Reva paid no heed. Griffon was in the lead, running at an angle calculated to intercept her as their paths converged. But he hadn't counted on the wall of underbrush separating them. Forced to stop, he cursed loudly and circled back. Jessica passed him, stumbled over a root and caught herself against the rough bark of a pine tree before she went sprawling.

"Stop. Reva, stop," she shouted. But her assistant ran on as if the devil himself were chasing her.

"She's heading toward the river," Jessica gasped.

Reva wove through the trees. Jessica pounded after her, hearing the roar of the water increase.

Suddenly, through the foliage, she could see the river, and she cried out in shock at the wild, surging expanse of dirty brown, spilling out of its normal course, carrying tree trunks along on its surface like matchsticks.

As if unaware of the danger ahead of her, Reva sped on. But Griffon had passed Jessica and was gaining on her.

Heart pounding, throat burning, Jessica stumbled forward. She could see Reva was heading toward a crumbling stone building that had probably stood well back from the bank. Now it was surrounded by slowly eddying water.

Was that why Reva had come here? Because she remembered that a vampire couldn't cross flowing water. Maybe she thought she'd be safe in the little house.

Jessica sighed with relief. The building wasn't in the main current. They could follow Reva inside and take her back to the mansion.

The terrified woman had reached the water. Plunging in up to her knees, she splashed her way to the building and disappeared around the corner. Griffon was a dozen yards behind her. And Jessica was at least that far behind him.

Another scream split the morning air.

Jessica stood frozen, her gaze trained on the house. Then she saw a flash of scarlet in the water. It was Reva's silk robe. Above it her red hair bobbed, and her pale arms seemed to claw at the air. The current grabbed her, sweeping her downstream.

"Matthew!"

Lurching to a stop, he changed course and began to run beside the surging river. But as Jessica watched in horror, a tree trunk swept downstream, rolled over Reva and swept her under the surface as if she had no more weight than a doll.

Jessica drew abreast of Griffon, panting and sobbing and praying that she'd see the scarlet robe bob to the surface. But there was no sign of it—and no sign of Reva.

"Oh God. Oh God," Jessica sobbed, hardly able to comprehend what had happened. "Somebody did this to her! Tricked her into killing herself! While we were in the carriage house trying to convict her of a crime she didn't commit!"

Griffon stared at the swollen river, as if he couldn't quite believe what they'd both seen. Before he could say anything, another voice floated above the sound of the torrent. "Reva…Reva…"

They both turned toward the frantic cry as Diedre stumbled into view. Her face was gray, bits of branches and brambles clung to her sweat suit, and her shoes were unrecognizable under a thick coat of mud.

Both Griffon and Jessica ran toward her.

"Reva…have you seen Reva?" She was panting.

"I'm sorry." Jessica choked out the words. "We couldn't stop her from plunging into the water." She gulped and forced out the rest.

"Oh, Lord."

"Neither one of us could catch her," Griffon added.

Diedre dragged in a shaky breath. "Neither could I."

"What happened? Why were you following her?" Griffon asked.

She sucked in more air before answering. "When I woke up, she wasn't in bed. I waited to see if she was in the bathroom or something, but when she didn't come back I threw on some clothes and went to look for her." The older woman puffed. "She was downstairs on the porch screaming and flapping her arms around her head as if something were attacking her."

"Like the bat that came at me." Jessica glanced at Griffon.

He turned to Diedre. "Could you see anything?"

"No. But she was screaming about the vampire." She looked pleadingly at Jessica. "Do you think—"

"No!" Jessica assured her, giving an abbreviated account of the last hour.

"Then I guess somebody did that to her, too," Diedre sobbed.

Jessica took the older woman into her arms, and they rocked together. Feeling Griffon's presence beside her, she looked up and caught the bleak expression on his face.

She held out her hand to him. "I was upset, and I made it sound like it was your fault she went into the river. It wasn't."

He hesitated before grabbing her fingers. She squeezed his hand and he came closer so that his other arm was around her shoulder. For several moments, none of them moved.

Then Diedre shuddered. "The others…back at the house. They could be in danger, too."

"We've got to come up with a strategy to protect ourselves," Griffon said. "Until we can get out of here."

Quietly they all started back.

The first thing they saw when they drew near the house was Heather pacing uncertainly down the steps and then back to the door. "Oh, thank God," she exclaimed when she saw them. Perry appeared on the porch, looking elaborately unconcerned, a steaming mug in his hand.

In the kitchen, Edward was hunched over the kitchen table, his head cradled in hands that trembled. Another coffee mug was in front of him, but it looked as if he hadn't touched the contents.

"How are you feeling?" Jessica asked.

He raised his head, and she stared at bloodshot eyes and skin that was a shade somewhere between putty-gray and evil green.

"Hung over and frightened," Perry answered the question for him, his voice contemptuous as he reentered the kitchen. "I've been filling him in on what he missed at the meeting last night. It looks like he's going to be about as much use to us as a dried-up can of paint."

Heather clutched Jessica's arm. "Where's Reva?" she asked.

"I'm afraid there's been an accident," Jessica answered gently.

"Tell me! Just get it over with and tell me!"

"Let's all sit down first." It was Griffon who spoke.

When everyone was seated around the table, he told them what had happened at the river.

"I knew it!" Heather whispered. "I heard her screaming, but I was afraid to get out of bed. It was the vampire. It's going to get us all, isn't it?" She turned to Jessica, her eyes pleading.

Perry snorted. "It's daylight, you stupid little twit. Vampires go back to their coffins when the sun comes out, so you've got a twelve-hour reprieve."

"Stop making yourself feel macho by sniping at everyone else." Griffon ground out the words.

The two men faced each other tensely across the table, and she waited to see whether Perry would back down. With an elaborate shrug, he got up and began to rummage in one of the drawers. He came back with a spoon, which he used to stir his coffee.

Jessica let out the breath she'd been holding.

Griffon gave her a half smile, and she tried to smile back.

He looked around at the circle of tense faces. "The first thing to do is to make sure everybody's up-to-date on information. We can start with what happened at the trailer this morning." He nodded to Jessica.

Wishing she didn't have to talk about it, she gave a matter-of-fact account of her visitation—and then of their search for and discovery of the bugs.

Heather looked around fearfully. "Then somebody could be listening to this conversation right now."

Jessica felt her scalp prickle as she and Griffon exchanged glances. All along they'd assumed that the culprit was one of the group, but Heather could be right. What if someone else had been here since they arrived?

"It's a big old house." Diedre voiced her thought. "There could be secret rooms, secret passages. Did you check that out before we moved in?"

"I'm sorry, I wasn't thinking about being stalked," Jessica answered.

Perry scraped back his chair and started for the door. "We'd damn well better think about it now."

"Don't leave. It's safer if we stick together. Reva got into trouble because she went off alone," Jessica told him.

Perry pressed his lips together, but he stayed in the doorway.

"The voice could have told her to drown herself!" Edward entered the conversation for the first time.

Griffon's sharp gaze focused on him. "Have *you* heard anything?"

The older man looked down at his hands, which were clasped tightly together on the table. The knuckles were white.

"Please," Jessica urged, "we're all in this together, and any scrap of information might be the thing we need to save our lives."

"I thought it might have been from..." His voice trailed off.

"Alcoholic hallucinations," Perry spat out.

Jessica shot him a sharp look, and he closed his mouth abruptly.

"Everybody's been experiencing weird things," she told Edward. "Like the make-believe vampire that visited me this morning. That was pretty frightening. And it's happened to other people, too. What did *you* hear?''

Edward cleared his throat. ''Well, I, uh, woke up in the dark and heard whispering. Someone directing me to get out of bed.''

''Did you?'' Jessica asked.

''Not bloody likely! I'm not going to let any voice tell me what to do, am I.''

''How did you make yourself ignore it?'' she persisted, hunching forward, her hands clutching her arms.

''I clasped my hands over my ears and squeezed my eyes shut—that's how.''

''Apparently Reva was more susceptible. She wasn't able to stop herself from being swept downstream,'' Griffon told the group, but his eyes flicked to Jessica.

She nodded, understanding the message. She had stopped following the commands. Reva had died.

''By the way, after Jessica left the bedroom, I could hear the voice that was talking to her,'' Griffon said. ''Did anyone else hear anything unusual last night? Heather? Perry? Diedre?''

Heather and Perry shook their heads.

Diedre looked uncertain. ''I'm not sure,'' she murmured. ''Maybe some of the whispering to Reva. Or my mind could have conjured it up.''

''But we know for sure that Reva was affected. So let's start by looking for a microphone in the room where the women slept.''

Quietly, as if they were afraid someone was listening, they all got up from the table and tiptoed toward the stairs upstairs.

Griffon led the way to the makeshift women's dorm. As the others filed inside, Heather touched Jessica's arm.

The young woman twisted her foot in a circle on the carpet. "This is making me, you know, nervous," she said in a low voice. "Is it okay if I hit the little girl's room for a minute?"

Jessica hesitated. "Come right back as soon as you…uh…" Her voice trailed off.

"Yeah."

Griffon looked at Jessica inquiringly as she entered the room. "Where's Heather?" he asked.

"Bathroom."

He nodded and continued with what he'd been saying to the little group. "The microphones we found in the trailer were flat disks about the size of a fingernail. They were both hidden in light fixtures. But they could be anywhere. Why don't we each take part of the room? That way, we can finish quickly. Diedre, you check out Reva's bed."

Perry, who was making an effort to cooperate, gestured toward the ten-foot-high ceiling and the light fixture. "You're not going to reach that thing without a step stool. There's one in the closet in my room—I guess for the top storage shelves."

"Would you mind getting it?" Griffon asked, matching Perry's conciliatory tone.

"Sure. Be right back."

Diedre and Griffon each took a quadrant of the room. Jessica started in one of the remaining corners, crawling along the baseboards and then feeling the edges of the window frame. Absorbed in the task, she'd been working for a while when she realized that neither Heather nor Perry had come back. Frowning, she glanced at her watch, wondering exactly how much time had passed.

Not wanting to alarm any of the others, she moved quietly across the carpet toward Griffon and touched his sleeve. "I'm going to check on Heather."

"Damn!" he whispered. "And Perry. Maybe we shouldn't have let anyone go off alone. Take Diedre with you and bring Heather back. I'll go see what's keeping the soap opera king."

Jessica couldn't stop her stomach from tightening painfully as she and Diedre made their way down the hall to the bathroom.

"Heather? Are you all right?" she called through the closed door.

The young woman didn't answer. In fact, no sounds at all came from inside.

"Heather?" Jessica rapped on the door. When there was no response, she glanced questioningly at Diedre.

"Better open it. She could have fainted or...or something."

With clammy fingers, Jessica turned the knob. The door was locked. "Heather? Are you all right? Heather?" she called out, banging on the wood and rattling the lock.

Footsteps came hammering along the floorboards, and Griffon was beside her. "What's wrong?"

She twisted the knob "Heather's locked herself in, and she doesn't answer."

Griffon rammed his shoulder against the barrier— once, twice. It gave, and the door flew inward.

The room was empty.

Chapter Fifteen

Jessica felt the hair all over her scalp stand on end.

"Heather!" she moaned, reaching out to steady herself against the sink.

Griffon cursed under his breath. "Perry's not in his room, either. I don't suppose he came back this way?"

Jessica shook her head.

"Heather! Perry!" he raged. "I've had enough of this. Get back here, both of you!"

The only reply was an awful silence hanging over the house.

Diedre began to tremble violently. "First Re-Reva. Now it's got Heather and Perry, too."

"Nobody's got them!" Jessica exclaimed. "They were here a few minutes ago."

"They can't have gone far," Griffon added.

Edward must have heard the commotion, because he came shuffling down the hall from the bedroom. "Maybe they're the ones," he rasped.

"The ones?" Jessica questioned.

"Doing all the hell-raising," he clarified. "And they've gone missing so they can play some more dirty tricks."

"No. Perry hates Heather," Jessica objected before reconsidering. "But they did pick the same time to disappear. And she's the one who shot down my theory about the scarf."

"The antagonism could be a ruse," Griffon said pointedly. "And Perry was being real cooperative all of a sudden. But we don't have time to waste debating it." Quickly he led a search of the upper and then the ground floor. They all went room by room, peering under beds, opening closets, pulling drapes aside and rapping on walls—looking for the missing pair and for secret passages.

Jessica's spirits sank a notch lower when they found nothing.

"We're all going to vanish, one by one," Diedre whispered. "Couldn't we just go upstairs and barricade ourselves in one of the bedrooms?"

"Heather disappeared from behind a locked door," Griffon reminded her.

"Well, I'm bloody well going to bolt myself in," Edward stated.

"You mean you're going to your room because you need a drink," Griffon clarified.

The actor turned quickly away.

"Please. We have to stick together," Jessica pleaded.

But Edward ignored her and stalked toward the stairs.

"We'll never see him again," Diedre moaned.

Griffon's face was bleak in the shadowy light. "Yeah. And maybe Reva was right."

"About what?" Jessica asked.

"About the vampire. About me."

"No!"

"I feel like I've stepped into one of my books," he said in a voice that rang through the empty rooms. "Nothing is what it seems. Next the walls will start to shimmer and dissolve."

He sounded like a man going to pieces under terrible pressure. Jessica moved closer to him, grabbing his hand and squeezing it tightly. "Someone's working very hard to make us feel that way."

"It's more than I can take!" He yanked her around so that she was facing him.

His whole demeanor compelled her to focus on his eyes. When he dug his nails into her palm, she caught the urgency of his gaze.

"We can't even talk because the vampire might be listening," he rasped. "It's like in the trailer. Before we went outside. Remember?"

"Yes." *When they'd concocted a fake little scene to try to put the hunter off the scent.*

"We can't make plans without somebody knowing every move we're going to make. So what the hell are we going to do?"

They stood staring at each other in the dimly lit hall.

"I understand…why you're so upset," Jessica murmured.

"Oh, do you?" he growled. But some of the tension had gone out of his face.

Now what? she mouthed.

Basement.

Jessica felt a ripple of fear slither over her skin. After finding Richie at the bottom of the stairs, she'd studiously avoided the cellar. But Griffon was right. It was the only place they hadn't searched. If Heather and Perry didn't turn up, there might at least be some clue down there.

Griffon squeezed her hand. Then he reached under the tail of his shirt and pulled out the revolver he'd packed in the knapsack.

Somehow the gun made her feel both safer and more vulnerable. Safer because they had a weapon. Vulnerable because it was an acknowledgement of unknown danger.

Jessica helped Diedre to her feet. The actress leaned against her as they made their slow way down the hall. "Where are we going?"

"Better not talk here," Jessica murmured, then looked around with exaggerated caution at the walls and ceiling as she cupped her hand around her ear.

Diedre's jaw tightened.

Griffon, who was a few paces ahead, stopped at the entrance to the basement and pressed a hand to Jessica's shoulder. She nodded, watching as he tested each of the stair treads before trusting it with his full weight. When he reached the bottom, he gestured for Jessica to follow.

The only way to make herself descend into the damp and darkness was to move quickly. So she fairly flew down the steps, feeling the cold, dank air reach out tentacles that wrapped themselves around her like some hungry, living thing. With all the rain, the walls seemed to ooze moisture, and the atmosphere was thick with the choking smell of hidden mold. Shivering, she crossed to Griffon.

"You're doing fine," he murmured as he pressed her close.

She gave a self-deprecating little laugh. "Oh, sure."

Diedre sank into a little heap on the bottom step. "How could Heather and Perry just vanish from under our noses?" Her voice cracked and Jessica knew she was on the thin edge of hysteria.

"They could have used a window."

"Maybe it isn't both of them. Maybe Perry followed Heather down the hall and grabbed her before she closed the door," Jessica suggested.

Diedre looked fearfully around the cellar. "It's not safe here. Why don't we leave the house?"

"And do what? Go where?" Jessica asked.

"But don't you feel it?" Diedre quavered.

"Feel what?"

"Evil."

Jessica gave a nervous laugh and struggled to get a grip on herself. "Don't fall apart," she urged, glad she had the job of bucking up Diedre. "Somebody's deliberately trying to make us come unglued, so we can't figure out what's going on."

The actress responded with a little sob.

"It's all right," Jessica murmured comfortingly. "We'll get through this." When she looked up at Griffon, he was standing near the steps, his head cocked to one side as if he were listening to something.

"What is it?" Jessica hissed.

"Don't you hear it?"

She strained her ears and thought she detected a faint grating noise that might have been coming from deep in the earth. It sent a shiver along her neck and down the length of her spine.

She had taken a couple of steps toward Griffon when everything was plunged into total blackness.

Jessica froze as she felt an unexpected rush of cold air whoosh toward her. It was followed by a scuffling sound. Diedre screamed and began to thrash around as if she'd been grabbed by a monster none of them could see.

Griffon bolted forward. In the darkness he slammed into Jessica. She clutched at him.

"Wait! Diedre!"

"She's gone."

They were both silent. Nothing moved around them. Jessica pressed her head against Matthew's chest so that she could feel the pounding of his heart. Dimly she realized that hers was thumping just as frantically.

"Diedre?" Griffon called out sharply. There was no reply. "Diedre, answer me!"

Still nothing.

He cursed, shifted his weight and fumbled for something. A narrow light pierced the darkness, and she realized he'd been carrying a small flashlight as well as the gun. Jessica anxiously followed the beam with her eyes as he played it back and forth across the floor.

Griffon tried to move past Jessica and into the cavernous reaches of the basement.

She clutched his arm. "Don't leave me alone. If— if you do, you'll disappear. Or I will!"

He turned back toward her and held her tightly.

She began to shake uncontrollably in the darkness.

"They're all gone. Vanished. If we go upstairs, Edward will be missing—just like everybody else."

"And we won't know whether it's because something has happened to him or if he's the one who's been playing nasty tricks. Maybe the drinking is an act so nobody would ask questions when he shut himself in his room."

"You said he was out cold when you went to get him for the meeting."

"That's what I thought."

Jessica closed her eyes against the darkness. Griffon's fingers stroked her shoulders and she felt his lips brush her hair.

"Why is this happening?" she whispered.

"I'd like to know."

"Well, the only thing I know for sure is that I didn't see anyone come down here or hear anyone drag Diedre upstairs. Which means whoever snatched her had to come from the other direction."

Griffon took Jessica's hand. "Come on, we're going to figure out which one of them is trying to drive us insane."

"Can't we just leave?"

"How far do you think we'd get? Outside we'd make great targets."

She nodded tightly, and he began to lead her farther into the midnight reaches of the basement. But she took only a few steps before the walls seemed to press in upon her. She dug her heels into the floor. "I don't want to go back there."

"Neither do I."

Reluctantly she let him guide her forward again. Yet

every taut nerve in her body was screaming for her to run in the other direction.

She fixed her eyes on the narrow flashlight beam, praying that it wouldn't go out. It was impossible not to imagine spooky things lurking beyond the little sliver of illumination, stalking her and Griffon, moving with them and dancing adroitly away when the light happened to swing in their direction.

"W-we need a better flashlight," she blurted.

"I know. But if we go get one, whoever's out there will have time to get away and set up the next ambush. And it will be for us."

Jessica glanced over her shoulder. They had come through several lightless rooms, and she wasn't so sure she could find the way back to the exit if the flashlight failed.

The realization added another layer of terror to the fear already clawing at the inside of her chest. Gasping for breath, she clutched Griffon's arm as if she were a blind woman set down in an unfamiliar place.

But even as she clung to him, the damp, inky blackness and the appalling feeling of being stalked began to do strange things to her mind. Gradually she passed into a realm where fantasy and reality blended. What if Griffon were the one? What if he'd been playing with her emotions all along? And this was the moment he'd picked to lead her to destruction?

When she hung back, he tugged on her hand.

The beam of light hit a cinderblock wall.

"Damn." Griffon let go of her hand and moved toward the wall. He played the light slowly back and forth over the surface.

Jessica exhaled a long sigh. "We can go back now," she said, feeling a profound sense of relief.

"No."

"Matthew, come on. Something bad is going to happen if we stay here."

Ignoring the warning, he stooped and ran his hand along the flooring. "I feel an air current."

"What?"

"There's air moving between this room and another one on the other side of the wall."

"But it's solid."

"It's supposed to look that way." Excitement ran in his voice as he set the gun on the floor and handed Jessica the flashlight. "Hold this while I see if I can find the mechanism that opens it."

Jessica wrapped her hand around the plastic case. She had the light. She could go back. Get out of this awful place. Somehow she forced herself to stand firm and hold the light while Griffon went over the surface of the wall, testing and pressing with his hands.

A grating sound brought the hairs on her arms to attention.

"Don't!" she gasped, knowing all at once that opening the secret door was the wrong thing to do.

"I've got it!"

Heart drumming in her ears, she backed away as she felt a rush of damp, chilly air.

Then something screeched high and piercing as it flapped out of the darkness. Only this time instead of beating its wings around her head, it dove for her neck, its sharp teeth sinking into her flesh.

Chapter Sixteen

Jessica screamed again and again as she dropped the flashlight and fought to pull the evil creature away from her. Something crashed to the floor and the light went out.

Dimly she heard Griffon say, "Wha—" But the word was choked off.

Finally she knocked the fluttering, clinging thing away from her body. Turning, she staggered into the darkness, clutching her wound. Her shoulder grazed a wall as she fled, and she cried out in pain. But the obstacle barely slowed her down.

A dim shaft of light wavered ahead of her, and she realized with heartfelt relief that it was coming from the door at the top of the stairs. Scrambling up the steps, she slammed the door and lay panting and sobbing on the hall floor. When she pressed her fingers against her neck, they came away bloody. As she gawked at the red streak, fear threatened to swallow her whole—to wipe every coherent thought from her brain.

Then a picture of Matthew flashed into her mind. She held fast to it with everything she had—yearning toward him, used his image to bring her panic under control.

Oh God. He was still in the basement. She'd run away and left him. Now she had to go back and help him.

Jessica stared down into the darkness and shuddered. Diedre had been right. Evil was lurking there. Evil beyond imagining.

Utterly alone, she hugged her arms around her shoulders and rocked back and forth like an abandoned child. She needed help. But she was the only one left in this godforsaken death house. The only one who could save Matthew—and herself.

MATTHEW'S EYES were closed, his body limp and boneless. He didn't fight as strong hands dragged him across the cement floor. He'd been startled when a needle had pierced his flesh. Then the rush had come—and he'd been swamped by a wonderful, familiar lethargy.

Worry, anxiety seemed to drift away on a pastel cloud. Gratefully he let them go. He had been on some mission that had seemed important. He'd been trying to keep everything from coming out wrong again.

But it didn't matter now. He felt too relaxed. Too peaceful. Too sleepy to worry about any worldly crisis.

It was just like after the accident. When the nurses had come with regular injections to take away the pain, and he'd found out he could drift away into a space of his own where nothing seemed important or urgent.

Sleep. Oblivion. That was the best thing. The answer to all his past and future problems.

Far away a door slammed. Or did it just sound that way?

Rough hands tumbled him onto what felt and smelled like a pile of musty rugs. It wasn't very comfortable, but he lay dreamy and drifting, his bones like jelly.

He sensed others in the room. Beside him someone was breathing heavily. Matthew's lids flickered just enough for him to see his companion. It was Perry, his body inert and his mouth slack.

"Go beddy bye, Griffon," a voice rasped. "Until I need you to finish out my plans. We've had the broken steps, the bats, and the hypnotism, the microphones, and all the rest of the special effects. It's all worked very well, even if you did find the bugs. Now we're almost ready for the grand finale."

He knew who was speaking. Sort of. He knew. But he couldn't quite remember who it was. And he didn't care. About the voice or anything else. Now that his wife was dead.

His mind twisted in confusion. His wife. Hadn't that been a long time ago? Long, long before he'd met Jessica—and fallen in love with her. Jessie. The woman who was meant for him. His own true love. Maybe she would come to him here, and they could drift through the clouds together.

He smiled.

"That's right. You think you're so clever, so intellectual. But I've got you where I want you. Like all the rest of these sleeping turkeys. And now I can finish with Jessica.''

He made a tremendous effort to speak. ''Vampire?''

''Wouldn't you like to know?'' The question was followed by a harsh laugh. Then there was only cold and silence.

NEED FLASHLIGHT. Need flashlight. Need flashlight.

Jessica chanted that over and over as she scrabbled frantically through the bags and boxes stashed in the pantry. Heedlessly she began tossing supplies in a circle around her. Napkins. Plastic bags. Cereal. Toothpaste.

Finally she found what she was looking for under a twin pack of paper towels. With the light clutched tightly in her hand, she started back toward the basement door.

Matthew had put down the gun so he could examine the wall. If she could find it, maybe—

She couldn't come up with any more of a plan.

With a little sob, she touched her neck. Truly she didn't know who or what she was fighting. All she could say was that a solid wall had moved, and Matthew had disappeared. And she had to find him or die trying.

Jessica never got as far as the basement door. She was halfway down the hall when shrill laughter stopped her in her tracks.

It was coming from above her. Around her. From below her feet, it seemed. She still grasped the flashlight as she pressed her hands over her ears. But it did no good. The sound wormed its way between her fingers, into her head, into the cells of her brain, like a viper's teeth.

"Stop. Please stop."

"Your wish is my command."

Instantly there was utter silence. Ominous silence.

Heart blocking her windpipe, Jessica backed away. Before she could take more than a half dozen steps, the dark shape of a bat came flapping out of the shadows, its wings beating the air as it swooped toward her.

IT HAD BEEN a long time since he'd felt like this. Safe and peaceful. Like rocking in a sea of half-formed dreams. Once he had craved this numb state, where pain was only a shadow flickering in a tiny corner of his mind.

Then an idea for a story had started dancing tantalizingly through his imagination, and he'd found to his horror that he couldn't summon the words to write it down. To this day he wasn't sure why the need to create had been stronger than the need to banish pain. But creation had won. That had been the first step toward winning his freedom. Of coming back to life.

He had traveled down an endless, dark tunnel. For a long time he hadn't even known he was still trapped inside the curving walls. Then he'd spied Jessie standing at the end—surrounded by light and hope and all the good things he'd told himself he didn't need. She was waiting for him. Calling to him. Urging him out of the darkness. And getting to her, holding her tightly, had become the most important thing in the world.

Jessie. Oh, God, Jessie.

He'd claimed her as his own. But it was going to happen again. Someone he loved was going to die.

The terrible knowledge was like a jolt of adrenaline to his system.

This time—this time he had a chance to save her, to make it come out right.

Summoning a superhuman burst of energy, he struggled to strip away the layers of foam that wrapped his mind. He'd been drugged by someone, but he knew how to fight the narcotic circulating in his bloodstream. He had done it before. Long ago, before he'd kicked his addiction. When he'd needed to be coherent.

Somehow he pushed himself to a sitting position and pulled his legs against his chest. Head cradled on his knees, he fought a wave of nausea.

Time passed. Maybe minutes. Maybe eons. When he opened his eyes, he found he was in a darkened room. A ventilator fan hummed in the ceiling. Around him were sleeping people.

Perry was beside him. The others?

Diedre and Heather lay on narrow cots along the wall. Edward looked as if he'd been carelessly tossed into a corner.

Perry. Diedre. Heather. Edward. All of them were here. In a drugged sleep. So who had made the basement wall move? Who had dragged them into this underground room?

Carefully he looked around the utilitarian chamber. Concrete walls and floor. Metal bunks. A shortwave radio. Shelves of dusty canned food with outdated labels, bottled water and other supplies lining the walls.

This was some kind of emergency storeroom—with beds. A disaster refuge?

And then it came to him. He'd seen pictures of places like this. It was a bomb shelter. Probably built in the 50s when the U.S. population had been told they could survive a nuclear attack by barricading themselves in the basement and waiting for the fallout to settle.

Moving as quickly as he could—which was like slogging through chest-high water—Matthew forced himself to a standing position. His vision blurred, and his head began to pound. Grabbing a top bunk, he waited for the world to stop spinning. Then he lurched over to Heather.

"Wake up!" he commanded, shaking her with as much force as he could muster. She was the youngest and the fittest. The first to be brought here and probably the first to be drugged. But he got no response from his attempts to rouse her. She'd had no defenses against the narcotic. In fact, he doubted whether she even knew what had hit her.

He wobbled over to each of them in turn. Edward was the one in worst shape. His skin was cold, his breath was shallow and he was completely oblivious when Matthew jabbed a fingernail into the side of his neck.

He'd been drugged after drinking alcohol—which was a deadly combination. If he didn't get medical help soon, he wasn't going to make it.

Matthew staggered over to the reinforced door. It was locked. In anger and frustration, he pounded his fists against the barrier.

THE BAT FLAPPED past Jessica, crashed into the wall, and plummeted to the floor. With jerky little sobs, she backed away.

"That was just to get your attention! Like I've been doing all along."

Afraid to turn yet knowing there was nowhere left to hide, Jessica found herself facing the pale, ghostly figure of a woman clad in a billowing white gown. Her skin was the color of chalk. Her lips a slash of crimson. And her face was that of Reva Kane.

Jessica tried to scream, but no sound came from her throat as she backed away. "You're dead. I saw you drown," she gasped in a high, thin whisper.

Reva gave a long, delighted laugh. "Yes. You saw me swept downstream. And now I've come back to haunt you," she snarled. "Just the way C. R. Adams haunted my whole life."

Jessica stood rooted like a statue, unable to move, unable to draw in a full breath, unable to comprehend the twisting and turning of reality as she stared at the apparition.

Reva. Back from the dead.

What did Reva—Reva's ghost—have to do with her father?

The spectral figure slowly raised and lowered her arms, flapping the flowing sleeves of her gown as if they were wings. With measured steps, she advanced on Jessica as if she were an avenging demon. "I'll drag you down to hell with me. The hell I've lived in since I was born."

On a choking sob, Jessica turned and stumbled away, hardly aware of where she was going as she picked up speed. But Reva stayed only a few feet behind her.

Somehow they ended up in the living room. Reva closed the distance between them, grabbing Jessica with inhuman force, spinning her around and around. Then she hurled her down so that she landed in a dizzy, terrified heap on the sofa cushions.

Her sanity near the breaking point, she stared up in horror at the white-clad figure hovering over her. "No, please," she moaned. "Why are you doing this? What did I ever do to you?"

"You took away his love and his money!" Reva spat.

Jessica gawked at her. "His love?"

"My father's. Your father's."

"Your father?" Jessica gasped.

"You lived with him in a Moorish palace on Mulholland Drive, with servants to take care of your every need. And I was stuck in a miserable shack in Monrovia with a mother drinking herself to death because the great C. R. Adams had gotten her pregnant and kicked her out into the gutter." Reva's face was close to Jessica's; her fingers circled her arm and dug into the flesh.

Her skin smelled unwashed. Her stale breath hissed in and out of her lungs.

Frantically Jessica tried to push her away. Even as she did, sensory evidence was piling up. The woman hovering over her was solid and real. Her body was warm, feverish. And all at once Jessica knew she wasn't fighting a phantom returned from the river.

This woman was as human and alive as she was herself. "It's you, Reva. You're not dead."

Reva jumped back, her face a twisted mask. One moment her right hand was empty. In the next it held a revolver.

For agonizing moments, she said nothing, and Jessica waited for her to pull the trigger and end the terror. Instead she began to speak. "Yes, I'm alive. I had a dummy ready with clothes just like mine. All I had to do was throw it in the water and stay out of sight."

"Wh-why?" Jessica stammered. "What have I ever done to you besides give you a job?"

"I made myself so tempting, you would have been a fool not to hire me."

"Why?" Jessica asked again, trying to keep her talking, conscious that she was facing a very dangerous woman who had already killed with impunity. But there had to be a way out of this. In rapid succession, her mind ran through every thriller she could remember where the innocent victim gets away from the crazed killer with the gun. God, if this were only the finale of *Indiana Jones,* and she could close her eyes while Reva was vaporized by evil spirits.

"My mother was a pretty little starlet who thought the great director loved her," Reva was saying. "She found out how much he cared about her when she told him she was pregnant."

"But—but I never even knew about you. And if I had, I wouldn't have wanted to hurt you. Why are you blaming me?"

"You got every good thing I should have gotten from him."

Now it was Jessica who laughed as she pushed herself up straighter. "You mean from a father who'd spank you if your room wasn't perfectly neat. A father who'd mock you at the dinner table. A father who never said anything to you that wasn't critical—unless a Hollywood reporter was listening."

"I don't believe you."

"It's true. Living with C. R. Adams was like living in a concentration camp where the commandant's word was law. Only the facilities were plusher."

Reva slapped Jessica's mouth in a stinging blow.

Crying out in pain, she cringed back against the cushions.

"Shut up! Shut up! I won't listen to your lies. I've been following your glamorous Hollywood life for years."

Jessica pressed her hand against her burning lips as she stared at the woman with the gun. Her eyes were wild. Her mouth a grim slash. Obviously her mind had been poisoned years ago by her mother, and facts weren't going to change it now.

"What have you done with Matthew?" she demanded.

"He's in cold storage, with the others. In the bomb shelter. That's one of the reasons this house was so perfect. I'm the one who suggested it to Richie—but I let him take the credit. It's isolated and it's got secret passages. When you set the place on fire, your lover and the movie cast will all roast alive in their underground tomb."

"When I what?" Jessica croaked.

"You're unstable. I told that reporter—Montgomery—all about it over the phone. That's how he knew the murder of that derelict was worth investigating. I gave him a lot of background on you. How your mental problems were inherited from your father. We even talked about how you might have set up the death to promote your vampire movie. How it just takes a vacuum pump and some tubing to exsanguinate a victim.''

"No!''

Reva ignored her. "It was like a sign from heaven when you got interested in *Midnight Kiss*. I was thinking how satisfying it would be to bring you down just when it looked like success was in your grasp. And the vampire motif was perfect! I even imported a vampire bat from South America—to go with the custom-made remote control models. I told the designer they were for the movie—even though *you* were only planning to show the shadow of the bat through the window curtains. He didn't know you were cutting every corner you could on this production. Mine are like those airplanes hobbyists fly. Only they have extra controls for the sound effects and the sharp little teeth.'' As she stared at the wound in Jessica's neck, a smile flickered around her lips. "I liked watching you come unraveled. It was fun trying different things. It would have been nice to see if I could get you to shoot Griffon. But my barbecue plans are just as good.''

Jessica moistened her lips. Reva was the one with mental problems—and years of resentment and frustration to fuel her sense of purpose.

"How did you know about the tape my mother

made?'' she asked as she stealthily moved the flashlight into a better position.

''I pretended I was writing a book on the great director C. R. Adams—and I interviewed former staff members and people from the studio.''

''Then you know the only person C. R. Adams loved was himself.'' Jessica couldn't stop herself from arguing.

''Don't try to distort the picture!'' Reva warned, the gun in her hand jerking ominously. It seemed she'd discounted information she didn't want to hear—and would keep discounting it. And she was becoming even more unstable. If Jessica didn't try something soon she was a dead woman. But the only ploy she could think of was one of the oldest tricks in the book.

''Matthew, thank God,'' she called, as if she'd seen him in the doorway.

Reva half turned.

It was then that a black, familiar shape came flapping through the doorway, screeching as it circled the room.

Both women gasped and flinched away. Then Reva suddenly seemed to remember the gun in her hand. Raising it toward the flying creature, she fired... once...twice. She must have missed, because the bat whirled, came around again and dived at her. Its wings tangled in her hair. Its sharp teeth clacked as they grazed her scalp.

Raising her hands and screaming wildly, Reva beat at the bat. Seizing the opportunity, Jessica slung the flashlight like a club. She saw it hit Reva's head, heard the woman cry out in pain and surprise.

"Down, Jessica. Get down."

The shout came from the doorway. And Jessica's heart leapt, even as she rolled off the sofa and onto the carpet.

It was Matthew. Somehow it really *was* Matthew.

Reva whirled. "Damn you. Damn you!" The curse was punctuated by a series of shots from the gun.

Chapter Seventeen

She heard the gun crack again and felt something hot shoot past her cheek.

Two more shots rang out—this time from Matthew's gun—and a heavy body thumped to the floor. Jessica's heart was in her throat as she rolled over. Reva lay sprawled on the carpet, obviously dead. This time for sure. Matthew was charging forward into the room.

"Are you all right?" They both shouted the urgent question at the same time.

Jessica scrambled up, and they met with near explosive force in the middle of the room. To her everlasting relief, she was in his arms and they were hugging and kissing feverishly and trying to talk all at the same time.

"Thank God you're safe."

"I love you."

He had said it, too. And she stared up at him in wonder.

He drew Jessica out of the room, away from the body on the floor.

"She said you were in the bomb shelter."

"Yes. They're all down there. Drugged. Sleeping."

"How did you get away?"

"Would you believe there's something good that came from having been addicted?" He swallowed hard. "I knew Reva had given me a narcotic because I recognized the effects—and I was able to fight them off. Mostly."

"Are you really all right?"

"I think so. But if I start to nod off, give me a swift kick in the rear."

"I'd rather give you a hug." And she did, clinging to him for a few seconds.

"How did you get out?"

"At first I was too foggy to do anything besides pound on the door in frustration. Then I found the lock mechanism. I guess Reva wasn't worried about a bunch of zombies mounting an escape."

"Reva was my half sister," she said disbelievingly. Her eyes seemed to stare, as if she was searching for answers, for reasons that would explain everything that had happened. "Oh, Matthew, you were right. She hated my father—my whole family."

"I heard her while I was sneaking into position with her bat." He held up the controller.

"How did you know how to operate it?"

"No problem, once I got close enough to one to see how it worked. You pick up a lot of miscellaneous information when you're a writer."

Jessica grinned. Then she sobered. "We're still trapped here."

"No. Reva had a shortwave radio stashed in the bomb shelter. I called the cops. They should have been here by now. I guess the flood has obliterated the usual landmarks."

"We'd better go down and see what we can do for the others."

"Right."

This time Jessica didn't hesitate at the basement steps. "I'm sorry. I didn't want to believe it was Reva," she said as they descended. "I trusted her."

"She planned this very carefully—for years, apparently. And she didn't leave much to chance. Remember I was wondering how the steps were broken. Well, I sent the wood to a lab and got back a report just before we came out here. Reva used acid to eat through them."

"More information you were withholding?"

"Would it have made you feel any better?"

"No."

"She'd even built up her strength enough to haul around grown men."

"That's right! I remember when I was carrying my luggage, she was picking up things I couldn't begin to lift."

"The most diabolical part of her scheme was making sure you were friends, that you'd rely on her."

"How could anyone play a role like that day after day, month after month? She killed a man and was planning to kill the rest of you all to drive me crazy and make me look like a murderer. How could anyone hate that much?" Jessica whispered. "If she'd only come to me—we could have been friends. We could have pooled our talents. Instead—"

"I guess wanting to get even with you must have

been fed to her with her mother's milk. She believed everything she heard, because she didn't have much choice.'' He sighed. "The traumas of childhood can have a disastrous effect on the rest of your life.''

She found his hand. "But you can get over them— with help.''

"Jessie—''

Now that they were safe she wanted to find out exactly what he was thinking. But they'd come to the entrance to the shelter. She gasped as she saw the drugged cast members strewn around the room like discarded cord wood.

Jessica covered them with blankets while she and Matthew waited for the police. Finally they heard the whir of helicopter blades and Griffon went up to direct the police and medical team to the shelter.

The drugged actors were evacuated directly to the hospital.

"I'll bet none of them will want to film the movie,'' Jessica murmured as she watched one of the medivac helicopters take off.

He pressed her close. "You might be surprised. But if they back out, I'll help you find replacements.''

She turned to him, her eyes bright. "You mean *you'd* go ahead with it?''

"Oh, yes. And I'm going to find you some real money, so you can stop operating on a shoestring. With all the publicity we're bound to get from this, the film should be a big hit. So with our next project, we can pull out all the stops.''

Jessica felt her stomach tighten. Matthew wanted to keep working with her. Would he agree to her terms?

While they waited for their transportation to come back, he led her into the den and closed the door. "Sometimes a man and a woman get together for the wrong reasons," he said.

Her heart stopped.

"I mean me and Gwen," he clarified in a hollow voice. "I can see now that the relationship wouldn't have lasted. But I wanted to cling to the tragedy of her death, because that was the strongest emotion I could feel."

"Why are you always so hard on yourself?"

"I'm being honest, finally."

She took him in her arms, and he nuzzled his lips against her hair.

"Jessica, I knew you were the right woman for me as soon as we started exchanging those dueling faxes. But, with my track record, I was afraid of getting involved."

"In this case, *not* getting involved would have been fatal. Reva was waiting for her chance to get me. Your being on the scene was the only thing that slowed her down and finally stopped her."

"You weren't doing too badly."

"I was too trusting to be a match for her. I needed you." She gulped. "But I do have a few reservations about the future."

He went very still. "Oh?"

Her heart had started to pound, but she went on quickly. "About our professional relationship. If we're going to work together after *Midnight Kiss*."

"What reservations?" he asked carefully.

"Well, happy endings are important to me, and in

your books, it doesn't always work out that way. What if in our future projects, I want to give the main characters a wonderful life together, and you don't see it that way?''

He let out the breath he'd been holding. ''I think I can be persuaded.''

''In real life? Not just in books or the movies?'' She watched his eyes. The eyes never lied.

His were like shining new stars. ''In real life,'' he said in a strong, steady voice.

''Oh, Matthew.''

''You name it. Marriage. Kids. A movie production company. A vacation house in Maine. A world-class camper. A—''

She laughed. ''All of those—for starters. And love.''

''Especially love.''

Epilogue

From the Baltimore Sun

Midnight Kiss Bites into Vampire Legend

Move over Dracula and Lestat. There's a new contender for the title of king of the vampires. You can catch him in *Midnight Kiss,* the extraordinary movie filmed right here in Baltimore, which opened in a star-studded world premiere at the Senator Theater last night.

Most novel-to-movie translations are destined to disappoint those who have already read the book. Not so with this fruitful collaboration between Jessica Adams, daughter of legendary film director Cedric Adams, and bestselling novelist Matthew Griffon. It isn't often that a novelist and director appear to understand each other so perfectly. Mr. Griffon wrote a script that preserves the plot and characters of his disturbing novel yet opens up the story with cinematic awareness. And Ms. Adams has brought his brooding prose to life in a series of telling images that will haunt the viewers as effectively as the author's words haunt the reader.

But as much credit for this fine film goes to the cast as to the author and director. Tom Carnegie, who plays the vampire, is the linchpin who holds the ensemble together. He took over the role from soap star Perry Dunmore, who left the cast due to conflicting contract agreements after production was delayed last March. It's hard to imagine anyone doing a more superb job bringing Mr. Griffon's antihero—who like the other characters remains nameless throughout the book and novel—to life. Blond and blue-eyed, Carnegie is the exact opposite of the dark destroyer whose obsidian gaze and coal-black locks are as much a part of the Dracula cliché as his fangs. Yet he manages to convince us that he *is* the embodiment of this tortured soul who feeds on his victim's emotions as greedily as their blood. And the depth of his performance perfectly conveys the vampire's moral ambiguity. In the end, we see him as much a victim as a destroyer.

Heather Nielson and Diedre Rollins play a mother and daughter who are seduced—if that is precisely the right word—in turn by the vampire. That the jaded, world weary mother and the dewy fresh daughter both fall under his spell is both the irony and tragedy of the movie. Judging from her performance, Nielson has a bright future ahead of her. And Rollins should win an Oscar nomination for best-supporting actress.

The only minor disappointment in the cast is veteran actor Edward Vanesco, who plays the husband and father as though he has wandered in from a production of *Sink the Titanic*. But he comes through when it counts, in the scene where he walks in on his wife in the arms of the vampire, and assumes he's interrupted a lover's tryst.

The film is as thought provoking as any of Mr. Griffon's books, although astute readers will note some subtle changes in the ending. And moviegoers will be glad to hear that he and Ms. Adams are already working on another project—a retelling of his *Last Train to Eden*. It's an inhouse collaboration since Mr. Griffon is rumored to have moved into Ms. Adams's highrise apartment.

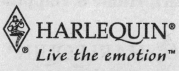

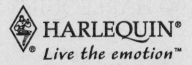

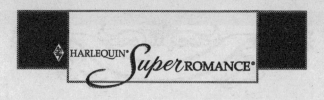

HARLEQUIN *Super* ROMANCE

...there's more to the story!

Superromance.
A *big* satisfying read about unforgettable
characters. Each month we offer *six* very different
stories that range from family drama to adventure
and mystery, from highly emotional stories to
romantic comedies—and much more! Stories
about people you'll believe in and care about.
Stories too compelling to put down....

Our authors are among today's *best* romance
writers. You'll find familiar names and talented
newcomers. Many of them are award winners—
and you'll see why!

If you want the biggest and best
in romance fiction, you'll get it
from Superromance!

Emotional, Exciting, Unexpected...

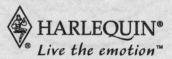

HARLEQUIN®
® *Live the emotion*™

Harlequin Historicals®
Historical Romantic Adventure!

From rugged lawmen and valiant knights to defiant heiresses and spirited frontierswomen, Harlequin Historicals will capture your imagination with their dramatic scope, passion and adventure.

*Harlequin Historicals...
they're too good to miss!*

HARLEQUIN®
INTRIGUE®
WE'LL LEAVE YOU BREATHLESS!

If you've been looking for thrilling tales of
contemporary passion and sensuous love stories
with taut, edge-of-the-seat suspense—then
you'll love Harlequin Intrigue!

Every month, you'll meet six new heroes
who are guaranteed to make your spine tingle
and your pulse pound. With them you'll enter
into the exciting world of Harlequin Intrigue—
where your life is on the line
and so is your heart!

THAT'S INTRIGUE—
ROMANTIC SUSPENSE
AT ITS BEST!

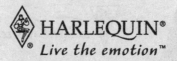

HARLEQUIN®
Live the emotion™

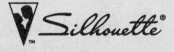

passionate powerful provocative love stories

Silhouette® Desire®

**Silhouette Desire delivers
strong heroes, spirited heroines
and compelling love stories.**

Desire features your favorite authors,
including

Annette Broadrick,
Ann Major,
Anne McAllister
and Cait London.

**Passionate, powerful and provocative
romances *guaranteed!***

For superlative authors, sensual stories
and sexy heroes, choose Silhouette Desire.

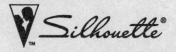

passionate powerful provocative love stories